THE REAL MacKAY

BOOKS BY

W. H. MURRAY

Mountaineering in Scotland
Undiscovered Scotland
Scottish Himalayan Expedition
The Story of Everest
Five Frontiers
The Spurs of Troodos
Maelstrom
Dark Rose the Phoenix
Highland Landscape
The Hebrides
Companion Guide to the
West Highlands of Scotland
The Real MacKay

A comedy in twelve chapters

THE REAL MacKAY

W. H. MURRAY

HEINEMANN : LONDON

William Heinemann Ltd.

LONDON MELBOURNE TORONTO
JOHANNESBURG AUCKLAND

First published 1969

© W. H. Murray, 1969

434 48202 1

Printed in Scotland by
Morrison and Gibb Ltd., London and Edinburgh

CONTENTS

CONTENTS

'Well, Donald,' I remarked one evening as we sat with our pipes over the peat fire, 'this must be a wild place in winter.'

'Oh, yess, sir, a wild place in the wintertime.'

'Big storms, I daresay.'

'Hoo, yess, storms.'

'And wrecks?'

'Ach, aye, wrecks, the weemens will be taalking about them whiles, but it will be years since she did not see any.'

'And strange animals, perhaps?'

'Heuch, aye, strange beasts and wild beasts.'

'Serpents?'

'Yess, serpents, aye and sea-serpents, creatt sea-serpents. There wass wanne, it wass two years ago, her head cam thro' the Kyle on the 7th of June, and it wass the 12th of August before her tail passed out. I wass tired waatching her.'

REVEREND A. E. ROBERTSON

AUTHOR'S NOTE

The subtleties of mind and character inherent in the people of any country are better portrayed through stories than by didactic analysis, which tends to obscure them. Yet I doubt if the West Highland Scots could ever have been intimately known from their heroic and legendary literature. Rich as the stock is, today it seems too formal and remote from our time. The humorous tales I tell here owe nothing to that tradition. They are altogether different in kind. I first heard them in West Scotland from 1938 onward, some at length, others in random fragments. I have brought this material together and dealt with it in my own way to give a comedy of life in a north-western village.

There are several distinguishing features in West Highland speech. The people do not speak broad Scots. They are Gaelic speakers, to whom English is a second language, which they use with a grammatical exactness and absence of elision not heard in purely English-speaking country. They make occasional mistakes, as do most of us in using a foreign tongue fluently. They use correct English pronunciation, overlaid with a soft sing-song that makes a true West Highland accent the most musical in Scotland.

The important peculiarity of their humour is a delight in exaggeration. They revel in it. The result can sound as wild as a witches' reel in Kirk-Alloway; it may caricature men and events, but it usually points up a truth, or emphasises a genuine human predicament. Their second trait is love of the romantic, ranging widely from landscape to human love or conflict; they will deliberately exaggerate to make joke of deep feeling, with the useful accidental effect that the reality at back of it all does not escape notice. While all this is true and can be valuable, basically they do it for the fun of it.

Before venturing fully into this wild literary land, I present two stories of its lairds. While there is no feudal relationship in a West Highland community, the life of the people is closely bound to the life of the landowner. Each of the twelve chapters could stand on its own, but I have loosely dovetailed them to give a continuing novel of adventures, mostly amorous and always romantic.

THE NEW EARL

I

On a spit of land, projecting into the sea at the head of Loch Screavie, stood Ross Castle. A splendid site it had. From the walls you looked right down Loch Screavie to the open sea, and beyond to the Western Isles. All the ground on the north shore belonged to Sir John Drumgast, including the village of Screavie, and all on its south to the Earl of Ewe, including Ross Castle.

Great was the excitement at Screavie when news came that the old Earl had died at sea on his way home from China. Little good had he ever been as neighbour or landowner, for his life had been spent abroad. Would his son and heir be any better? The lad was twenty-four, named Simon, Lord Frewin. His mother had died giving birth to him here in the castle. He had come back to it every summer since boyhood for long holidays, at first in care of his grand-uncle, old Jacob Frewin of Screavie House, but always these last five years with young women for guests. The ladies came and went, came and went, new ones all the time. Wullie the postman would be spending hours on his rounds down at Screavie, regaling folk with the gossip.

'Och,' say they, 'now he iss Earl he will be settling down.'

Sure enough, he did come to live in his castle, but during the next two years 'settling down' was not the name for it. The only change was that instead of having his women come to him he went to them. He was forever on the move, off to London, to Edinburgh, and to every county in the Highlands where there was a party, or ball in a big house: drinking, dancing, shooting, fishing, and making love to every girl who would let him. Few gave him a No, it was said. He was handsome and had not yet gone dead behind the eyes. His free and generous manner went down well with the ghillies—even them. They could see from his face he was in fair way to be decadent, but that time was not yet —and the women liked the look, so long as the man was still young.

As time went on the factor at Inverness grew demented. 'The estate is being neglected something shameful,' said he to Jamie Urquhart, the head keeper. 'You talk to him, Jamie. He'll take anything from you. Someone's got to tell him. Say that I asked you to speak.'

Jamie was nothing loth. He was not one of your quiet-spoken keepers, disliking to say what a man will not want to hear. He was a dragon, breathing fire and smoke when he felt the ghillies were needing it, and bold and bluff in dealing with masters. One morning, when the Earl had come back to the castle for a day or two, he marched into the morning-room after breakfast.

'I'm here at the factor's wish, my lord,' said he, fixing the Earl with an eye as stern as the Minch in a gale, 'to ask you to mend your ways if you will. A good landowner iss a blessing to man in the Highlands. The land takes heart. Every living thing takes a nourished look. But this Screavie estate cannot afford you, my lord. What's left of your forest iss dying of sheer neglect. The ferms and steadings are in ill plight and you'll not look at them. The factor tells you in plain terms and you stuff his letters in the waste-paper basket.'

'Not "stuff" them, Jamie.' Simon put on a shocked

2

expression. 'I drop them in—gently and never without regrets.'

'My lord, what you say and what you do are often different things.'

'Then think on this: neither I nor you can argue with death duties. At present they drain the estate. My sale of the north half to Drumgast failed to clear them. My long-term intentions are good.'

'Chust that! Man, why are they not good now? Now iss the time to be acting, not gallivanting perpetual. Men, weemen, and children live on your ground. Why not be giving them a wee piece of the consideration you lavish on weemen?—not only those fancy ones from London, but aal the rest. Iss there a high-born lass this side of the Highland line who hass not had a kiss from you? Haff you effer shaken a Screavie tenant by the hand and given ear to his troubles? My lord, you haff not—nor effer lifted a finger to help. Chenerous you are in talk, but in action—? No, not with discreemination. The money spent on lasses alone would haff fenced the forest. Aye, and the ferms. Man, they would haff come alive!'

'Jamie, you sound as though you'd never been in love.'

'I would not be calling it luff, my lord, when it means aal the weemen there iss and more.'

'Why not?' His lordship lifted a quizzical eyebrow and laughed.

The subject had to be dropped. As far as could be seen, Jamie might have saved his breath. The Earl was away that very day and not seen again for a fortnight. Things drifted on just as before. But one day in April back he came once more, pale in the face, languid, and tired, tired in the eyes. Not a bite would he eat for lunch. All that afternoon he moped in his own rooms. It was evening before he came outside, wandering round the walls like a ghost. In half an

3

hour he marched back to his room and threw himself down in his chair. He was wishing the castle would sink into Loch Screavie and himself with it. He had never been so bored, thought he, bored to screaming, since he had been to his own wedding. He sat up on that thought. It was little wonder that Jamie had clean forgotten that the Earl was married when he only remembered it now himself. For seconds he hesitated, then pressed a bell.

Old Janet Dunbar, the housekeeper, went up herself. On the Reverend MacLeod's advice, when his lordship rang she kept the lasses below stairs—and there he was, sitting with his head in his hands, hair over his eyes, and despair on his face. He perked up as she came in. 'Janet,' said he, 'is the Countess at home?'

'I would not know. But aye, she iss in the house.'

'Has she guests?'

'She iss alone. Back this morn from Edinburgh.'

'Go to her, please. Say that if she's free I'd like to call in half an hour.'

Janet started and shot him an anxious look. 'Your lordship will not haff taken leave of his senses? . . . Merciful Mother, this hass not happened in my time!' She bustled out, all agog to consider what was afoot.

Shuna, the Countess of Ewe, was the only daughter of a motor car manufacturer. Seven years ago, she and Lord Frewin had been married under strong parental pressure. She was eighteen, then, and not unwilling, for she had liked the look of Simon. For his part, he had been well-nigh press-ganged into wedding her as a duty to his ancient family: persuaded at the age of nineteen against his will, and ever after fiercely resentful. The girl's money, for which the old Earl had angled, came so tied up in trusts that the Ewe estates won never a pound. Lord Frewin cared nothing for that. The estates could go to the devil. Love not land was what he wanted. He had never bedded the lass. They had led their own lives from the start, slept in separate rooms, kept to their own friends, and at Screavie, when he came to the earldom, lived in separate halves of the castle. At no kind of social function were they ever seen together, and equally, if they met by chance, took no step to avoid each other. Neither could have cared less.

Once out of her teens, Shuna had grown in beauty, and not a little in wit. She soon had no lack of young men about her to spare the Earl the trouble of pleasing her. She managed these affairs better than he, for Wullie the Post could pin nothing on her. Gossip there was in plenty, but never evidence. She was in much demand all over the counties, and no more often at home than his lordship.

Janet found her mistress reading quietly by the fire. 'His lordship says to present his compliments,' she said, tossing her head. 'Believe it or not, he iss wanting to come and see you in half an hour, if you don't say no.'

'You mean my husband?'

'Himself, no less.'

'Janet! Has something terrible happened?'

'Aye, maybe. He's dishevelled-like.'

'You mean, drunk?'

'No, no! He's never seen the worse o' drink, ma'am. I mean he had a scunnered look on his face. My opeenion is, he's at his wit's end to know what to do with himself, but what else there might be I dare not say.'

'You might be right, Janet.' Her eyes twinkled. This could be amusing. 'Never did I guess he's come to such a pass. Give him my answer: I'll see him if he comes at six.'

In half an hour he was at the door. To Shuna's surprise he was wearing the kilt, a yellow waistcoat, and a jabot at the throat. He was immaculate—and very handsome.

'It is most kind of you—of your ladyship,' he amended

5

with a wry laugh, 'to see me at short notice.' He held out his hand, which she took coolly.

'Won't you sit down—my lord.'

'If I may, for a few moments. Your engagements allow?'

'They allow. You yourself must be short of time.' She eyed his clothes. 'A party at Inverness?'

'I'm sick of parties, and every other function you could put a name to. My visit to you is occasion enough.'

'Then I ought to feel honoured. Like you I'm weary of the social round—call it a whirl rather, for it makes me less sick than dizzy. It would be good to be at rest here, if one could.'

'You too?' He felt surprised, then looked around. 'Yes, your room does look like a haven, where no storms come. You have it beautifully furnished, Shuna—may I call you Shuna?'

'When one stops to think, it seems slightly absurd not to—Simon?'

'Please do. . . . As I was saying, your room's beautiful, happy atmosphere, neither formal nor slick—comfortable is the word. A room to relax in. . . . Now, tell me what you've been doing with yourself these last two years?—sorry, that's a bit much to cover all at once. Let's start closer. I've been in Rome for a week or two, and hear you're just back from Edinburgh. What's afoot in the capital?'

Formal as the start was, the conversation grew less stilted and became easy as each found that the other shared certain interests. Shuna had discovered new delight in chamber music: Simon in opera. He had developed a new concern over the emigration of Highlanders: she in the problems of attracting local industry. She preferred to ski in France, he in Switzerland. They discussed, argued, grew lively in mutual enthusiasms. Two hours had fled before they knew it.

6

'Good lord,' said he—'nearly eight o'clock: would you mind if I stayed for supper? Would I not be too troublesome?'

'Stay if you'd like to, Simon. I find I'm enjoying your company.'

He stayed. They ate. The talk grew lighter and their eyes gayer. He told his best stories, which she had never heard before, and sometimes, but not too often as yet, she capped them. Each felt his and her personality expand in this sympathetic atmosphere. They blossomed and refreshed each other, and were still not tired when they heard midnight strike on the clock in the hall.

He rose to go: 'I'd no notion it was so late. I do hope I haven't kept you too long out of bed?'

'Not at all. I could even say you've shortened the winter.'

They laughed. He looked at her, at those warm cheeks and shining eyes—but no, the time was not yet. He bowed and retired. That night he slept as he had not slept for eight years—lightheartedly.

In the morning he was up early, but downcast at breakfast on finding himself alone again. It was a day of wind and sun. He spent it fishing for sea-trout, and came home at four o'clock with a thoughtful look in his eyes. He rang for Janet, and when she came, 'Janet,' said he, 'I am supposed to be in Ullapool tonight, to speak at a political meeting for the Liberal candidate. I want you to ring up and say I'll not be there.'

'What ails your lordship?'

He coughed, and clutched his heart.

'Pleurisy,' she diagnosed. . . . 'My hands are full of invalids. Her ladyship's newly rung the provost of Inverness to say she can't come to his banquet.'

'Is she ill?'

'Aye. Pains about the hert.'

'Then I must visit her. Duty requires it. Janet, tell her I'll be along at six o'clock. But don't say a word of my pleurisy. I don't want to cause her worry on my account.'

'Simon, how kind of you to look in again!' exclaimed Shuna at six. 'I'm so glad to see you in your old tweeds—for that means you can stay to supper. You will, won't you?'

'I'd love to, Shuna. Quite free of engagements.' He looked around. The room was full of flowers. 'But what of you, Shuna? You have many friends calling here, I know. I shouldn't like to butt in.'

'I've no one else coming tonight.'

'Shuna, you're not really feeling out-of-sorts?'

'Why should I? Never better. I'm not a woman who must always have company in. Often I like to be alone. Tonight is different though—unexpected—a live husband! . . . Just look at the flowers, Simon. I do wonder who sent them. They came in from Inverness this afternoon.'

'You must have many—admirers, shall I say?'

'You may call them that. A few, I suppose. But lovers, no—not at present. No one has won my heart.'

'Don't bluff me, Shuna! You are twenty-six—'

'I know, I know. . . . There was one, perhaps, but that was a long time ago.'

'It would seem you still have one,' and he looked again at the flowers.

'I'm not aware of it. But won't you sit down? Tio Pepe on the side-table. Please help yourself. Tonight you look the picture of health, compared with yesterday. There's a bloom on your skin. Were you out on the hills?'

'Fishing. Sea-trout. Have you ever tried your hand?'

'No. Is it very exciting?'

'I'd love to teach you. You've no idea what a thrill it is when you hook a fighting fish.'

8

He was launched. There was never a dull moment that night. Each was rested and keyed up to give his and her best. Shuna's abounding liveliness poured out like sunlight, giving sparkle to his own wit. By the time supper was over they were openly admiring each other.

'I just cannot understand,' said he, 'how I've missed the change in you during the last eight years. When we met first, you seemed to me as cool as a douche—no passion for anything—no interest even in men. Now you're one hundred per cent alive.'

'You mean physically, I suppose?'

'I mean in mind, spirit, and body too.'

'We've done no more than talk. How can you know?'

'Then let's do more than talk—I can see the fire within the face: there's kindness in the eyes, fullness in the lips, generosity in the mouth, fearlessness in the way you carry the head. You're a woman. When did this change occur?'

'I've been asking myself the same of you, Simon. When was *your* change? I thought you immature—to be blunt, decadent. Now I see you're not, nor ever have been. What you did has never really touched you. You played a part not your own. Now you're yourself again. Why and when?'

This inquiry kept them talking till the clock in the hall again struck midnight. He rose. 'In your company, Shuna, an hour goes like a split second. If anyone had been listening he might have thought we were—'

'What?' she asked softly.

'I have it in me to feel sorry we're husband and wife.'

'Why do you say that?'

'We might be lovers instead.'

'Oh, please don't be sorry. I think your marriage has greatly improved you, beyond all reasonable expectation.'

'My marriage, indeed! Don't forget your own, Shuna.'

He stood still, reluctant to go. 'We must be off to bed.

Shuna, in the morning, let's have breakfast together. Would you mind? It would put a new look on my day.'

'Then let's! Nothing could be nicer. By the way, it *was* you who sent me the flowers?'

He nodded, still standing by the door, still reluctant to go. 'It's a pity our rooms are so far apart,' he sighed. 'Wish it were my bed too next door.'

She favoured him with a chaste smile, but no other light shone in her eye. 'I look forward to breakfast. Good night, Simon.'

Like it or not, he had to go, swearing softly, back through the long draughty corridors to his own quarters. 'She's entrancing,' thought he. 'Flat in the belly and lithe as a tigress.' And what she was thinking, no man might guess. But first thing in the morning she had a word with Janet. 'Janet,' said she, 'the master and I have spent two evenings together, and this morning we breakfast. Now, pay attention —I want no gossip, so not a word of this to Willie the Post.'

'I'll not breathe a word to mortal soul,' whispered Janet, her eyes afire to spread the news. Oich! the entire village was knowing already, saving the snippet about breakfast, and what more was that?

Breakfast proved a great success, the two of them lively as sparrows, just as if they were meeting for the first time. 'Shuna,' said he, 'there's snow in the corries of An Teallach. Will you come and ski?' She was blithe to reply, and this time she herself invited him to dine at night in her rooms. All day long they were away together and not back till seven.

That night it was a dinner for an Earl she had laid on, with the coals banked high in the fireplace, the servants trooping in and out with courses, and with wines to go with them. Her Simon had never eaten a meal like it in Castle Ross.

Strange to say, the talk was slow and less bright this evening. In spite of the wine, they seemed almost shy. The servants were wondering if the flush on their cheeks was just the sun and wind. They appeared to have run out of things to say. A good fire had been laid in the drawing-room too, but when dinner was over they never looked in there. Before the table was cleared the pair had vanished. Janet saw the light under the mistress's bedroom door, but she was not one to trust to mere speculation. She went later to the master's room for orders, but he was not there. She had tea sent up to him before eight in the morning, but his bed was empty. Indeed, he never slept there again.

Before long, Simon and Shuna were going everywhere together. It was the talk of the county. Never were they seen apart. Here is another strange thing. For all the time he lavished on his wife—more than ever he had on lasses from Lowlands or Highlands—yet, from now on the estate was left short of nothing. Its land and people were seen to flourish as never before.

BLACK-EYED SUSAN

2

GREAT was the love Sir John Drumgast had for his money, since he had made it himself, and though it was more than ever he could spend, a tight-fisted man he was. Like many another of his kind, he could be generous to guests and kindred, while hard, hard to the tenants and keepers on his Screavie estate. Quick to note any good points in his ghillies, never would he say he knew, lest they dream of a rise in pay. But he was kind to animals, so long as they were not human.

A day came when the feet were taken clean from under him, but you would never guess who managed that. The month was August, and a good one for a change. Drumgast had let out the shooting in Glen Buie and Glen Dorcha. These had lodges of their own, where the people stayed. He kept Glen Mhor for himself. Glen Dearg, which had no lodge, he had let to an American, Mr Timothy Tyler, who stayed with Drumgast at the big house. Tyler was one of the Texan oil kings, a long loose-limbed python of a man, with a belly on him and thin, sandy hair. He had never been to Scotland before, let alone Wester Ross, so he was thinking that Johnnie Drumgast was a Highland chieftain—and he a Fifer with not a word of the Gaelic.

Sir John liked the notion well and played to the gallery. He had the hall of his house hung with his coat of arms (motto in Gaelic), and with claymores, muskets, targes, and stags' heads. Always in the shooting season he wore the kilt and had a piper to play outside the window at dinner. At breakfast he supped his porridge standing, from a wooden bowl with a horn spoon, while he strolled around the room and took a bit look at the moors, or warmed his backside at the fire. Aye, well he knew how to pour the cream for rich Americans; they lapped it up purring, thinking this was high life in the Highlands, and Himself the greatest chieftain of them all. For the honour of knowing Sir John, being intimate with a real knight and a clan chief (who had no clan to his name), and being able to go home and show the lantern slides, they paid through the nose—over and above what they paid for grouse, stag, or salmon.

This August night, Mr Tyler and Sir John had finished dinner early and were sitting before the log fire discussing whisky. This subject was the great enthusiasm of Johnnie Drumgast's life. He knew it better than anyone. When he spoke it was an education to be listening. The production of whisky was not a trade, nor just an art, but a fine art. He would tell you all its history, and all the qualities to look for, and the merits of one malt or blend against another at different seasons of the year or time of day. And there on the table before them were thirty bottles of pure malts. Slowly, slowly, with careful study, they were working their way through the lot, just a thimbleful here and a thimbleful there—an abstemious man was Johnnie, never seen the worse of his whisky, for that would have spoiled his palate. Still and all, by the time they had sat an hour their spirits were rising. Sir John felt a glow tingle through his limbs, and Mr Tyler a lofty detachment from human frailty.

They had just agreed that two hundred bottles of Scotch would be a good start to a cellar, and cater for every mood (if well selected), and they were planning this very start to Mr Tyler's cellar in Texas, when a piercing whistle was heard outside the window. Tyler started. Sir John jumped to his feet. 'Man alive!' he cried. 'It's nine o'clock. That will be Angus whustling-in Susan. I'd clean forgot. Come you out and see this.' And out the two of them went.

This Susan was a roe-deer fawn. And Angus was Angus of the Glens, who had come from Screavie a year ago to take the job of Sir John's ghillie. His real reason was to be near Flora of Glen Mhor. In early spring Angus had found the fawn abandoned in the woods behind the laird's house. Sir John was delighted and weaned her on the bottle with his own hand. He called her Susan, because of her great black eyes. She had the run of the woods and the policies, and always wore a yellow collar, so that none of the keepers or ghillies might shoot her. Wherever she might be, Angus had only to whistle and she'd come. Every night at nine o'clock—by the laird's command—he would come to the terrace before the house and whistle, for no laird could whistle like Angus. Then Drumgast would feed her, and stroke her, and give her all the tender words that he never used on man, woman, or child.

Mr Tyler was enchanted with the scene he saw and the tale he was told. Susan took some grain out of his own hands. They felt her muzzle on their palms, softer than fur, and looked into her bright eyes, and stroked her head and neck and felt the velvet smoothness of her long ears. Aye, she was a bonny beast was Susan.

'I'd no' exchange the lass for a' the whusky in Scotland,' said Drumgast. 'She means mair to me than ma twa dugs, she's that graceful. Look at the way her snout trembles on the sniff, and the alert balance! Did ever ye see sic a swiftness in poise? It's more than a bird has. . . . Aye, if ever a man puts shot or bullet in Susan, he'll ha'e nae mercy o' me.

14

I'd gralloch him. . . . Och, but she's safe with you, Angus. Look after her weel, ma lad.'

The two men stood in the gloaming and watched Angus lead Susan to the back of the house, where he opened a gate to release her into the woods.

'Don't you fear poachers?' asked Tyler.

'Nay, nay, there's no' a poacher in Screavie would shoot the beast. She's safe wi' that yellow collar. They a' ken her fine.'

'But these ghillies, now,' said Tyler. 'They haven't the fine feelings of you and me. They're as tough, hard-swearing a set of thugs as I ever clapped eyes on in Texas. By heaven, they even have the neck to answer me back!'

Johnnie Drumgast bristled. 'Ye maun treat them as equals, else they'll no' work.'

Tyler's eyes widened. 'Will one of them not lay Susan down for his larder?'

'Na, na—they're my own men, and they're honest. Tak' that Angus, for example, the most honest man ye'd meet on earth. He'd no' touch a thing not his own. If he did, he'd tell ye. Susan's safer here than she'd be in a zoo.'

Tyler raised a supercilious eyebrow. 'That's not my own experience of men, Sir John. I made a billion dollars by learning to trust no man.'

'I made the like,' said Drumgast, 'by knowing who I *could* trust. For example, I'd no' trust you, and maybe that's a compliment. I ken weel what I'm aboot.'

'You're not realistic, chief,' sighed Tyler. 'Every man has his price. I'd bet Angus would spin a lie the same as you and me if it paid him. If he doesn't, it's just that he sees nothing to gain.'

Drumgast could never suffer contradiction. 'If it's a bet you want,' he snapped, 'I'll tak' ye. You get Angus to deceive me and tell me a lee. Just you try. . . . How long will ye need for that?'

'Three days. Give me a week, since I've still to get the lie of the land. . . . What will you want for stake?'

'Twa hunner bottles o' Scotch.'

Each man's eye brightened at the notion. They grew friendly again, each sure of himself. Back they went to the table. Agreed: that Drumgast must give no hint of the test to Angus, or to any other person. Agreed: that Tyler be free to use as many folk as he liked, so long as none gave Angus a word of warning.

'I sample your whiskies with noo keenness,' said Tyler. 'This tasting is filling a great gap in my edoocation.'

'It's about to fill a great gap in my cellar, I'm thinking,' grinned Sir John.

First thing next morning, Tim Tyler had a close session with his secretary, Johan Redebreest, whom the ghillies called Cock Robin, or Cocky for short. A burly lad, sure of himself in a way you never yet saw in a young Scot. Yet the eyes were sly. He had a way with the women, though, always flashing a smile that was never meant.

Tyler told what had passed betwixt him and Drumgast. 'The knight thinks he knows more about men than Tim Tyler of Houston, when the one thing he knows is whisky. I warned him: men are the same the world over. As in Texas, so in Ross. If you can't trust a servant one inch there, you can't here. . . . Look at me sideways if you like, Johan, but spare me the pained expression. You serve me well: I make sure it pays you. Well, now, any bright ideas? Out with them!'

'If you want to seduce a man, Mr Tyler, the quick way is through a woman.'

'Full marks, Johan! Do you keep the Good Book at your bedside? You've said what the Devil knew when he went to Eve first, not Adam. . . . Out you go, then, to the highways and byways. Try the house-servants first. If Angus has a woman, search her out. Learn what you can. Make a plan. The stake is five hundred pounds. Win me the bet and I'll pay you one hundred. I'll look an almighty fool if I lose— and that won't help you, son.'

While his master and Johnnie Drumgast were out on the moor, Johan spent a profitable hour gossiping in the kitchen. Soon he had the whole tale about Flora of Glen Mhor: how Angus had been crossing the Bealach Ruadh on Sundays from Screavie, how he had taken the job of ghillie just to be near her, how they had come to an understanding but were not married yet for lack of a house.

That very same afternoon, Cocky went scouting up Glen Mhor. As always, the Devil looked after his own, for he met Flora on her way to gather the last of the year's cut peats. He knew her at once—she of the hair brown as a roe-deer's, he had been told, the skin like foam on the ebb tide, and the eyes of her dark as a burn in spate. They stopped to pass the time of day. Cocky said who he was and asked if she was Miss Flora Macrae. She nodded, shy-like.

Cocky flashed her one of his Dutch smiles and lied, 'I've been having a word with Angus. A fine upstanding man he is. Says he can't get a house. Is there none hereabouts would suit him? Is there not one to rent?'

He could not have put his question better. It knocked the fetters clean off Flora's tongue. She could speak freely of this to a man not of her country.

'This very meenute there iss one that would suit us fine— over at Screavie there, on the other side of the hills. But the laird iss refusing to let. Says he, "It's for sale, not letting," the mean stirk he iss, for he rented the house to the last man there. It iss black burning shame he should think of himself, denying his own people the chance, and him with aal the money in the world.'

'Has he put a price on it?'

'Indeed, yess. Three hundred pounds.'

'Only three hundred? Are you quite sure? Surely that's not much?'

'It iss far more than enough. There iss no electric light, and no water inside, and new floors needed. Och, but it would be perfect for Angus and me. He would soon put in the floors and water: a right handy man iss Angus.'

'He can't raise even three hundred?'

Flora shook her head sadly.

'How short is he?'

'He could pay chust half.'

'Cheer up, Miss Macrae. The house is yours.'

Flora gasped. She dared not believe. Fright showed in her eyes while she stared into Cocky's self-assured, smiling ones. She saw their shallowness. 'To say that iss not chust teasing, Mr Redebreest, it iss cruelty. Go your way and leave me be,' and she made off along the track.

Cocky was after her in a flash. 'I mean it, Miss Macrae. Mr Tyler is ready to put down the money.'

At Tyler's name she stopped. She listened.

'Mr Tyler wants to buy the roe-deer fawn from Angus. He will pay a hundred and fifty pounds for it.'

'He will pay *what*? . . . But Susan iss not Angus's. She iss Chonnie Drumgast's.'

'Angus found it, did he not? He looks after it. Anyhow, Drumgast won't sell and Mr Tyler is set on having it. Drumgast need never know: he'd think it had run wild, or been shot by a poacher. But the house would be yours. Think how long you've waited—'

'Aye, four years. . . . Angus would never do this.'

'Think it over. What is a roe-deer fawn—to the happiness of man and wife in a wee house at Screavie? Angus will never hesitate—if he really wants to marry you, that is. . . . Meet me here tomorrow at the same time. I'll bring the money. I'll prove I'm in earnest. Think it over meantime.'

Flora watched his retreating figure with tears in her eyes. Four years is a long time in the life of a young woman. Maybe four more would stretch ahead till Angus found a house. And here was the money offered—'chust for one roe-deer' (she must stop thinking of it as Susan)—a gift from Heaven. It was the answer to all the prayers she said morning and night. If it was not all a hoax. Maybe no woman should rely on that Cocky Redebreest. He was not to be taken in earnest. The dream faded, and again the tears came to her eyes.

When Cocky reported that night, Tyler was well-nigh jumping for joy. 'It's in the bag!' he cried. 'Well done Johan! This very week we'll stand on the terrace and hear Angus whistle-in the fawn, and none will appear, and then we'll be hearing the lies come thick and fast. How much do I pay for that house at Screavie?'

'Three hundred pounds, Mr Tyler.'

'I never knew one could buy a house that cheap. I'll add one hundred for you.'

He sat down and wrote the cheque. 'Cash this at Inverness in the morning. I'll make one hundred profit on the whisky and humble this Scotch knight to the dust. This is better than shooting grouse, Johan—better even than stags.'

'You can mount Susan's head in your own hall back home, Mr Tyler.'

'Haw, haw! Haw, haw, haw!'

Cocky met Flora next day as arranged. 'I have the money,' said he.

'I haff the misgivings,' said she. 'Neffer in his life has Angus cheated a man. It iss not me that would want him to start.'

For answer, Cocky fetched from his pocket thirty new five-pound notes. He counted them out before her eyes.

'It's your own wee house you see in my hand. A life-time of happiness, with the man who loves you. See him tonight. Ask him to bring me the fawn tomorrow after the day's shooting is over. Make it seven o'clock at night. I'll have a van on the main road by the main gate. The fawn will go to Sandy MacTavish at Screavie, till we get her a berth for Texas. No one here will ever know. It's safe. Angus will do it if he loves you. If he won't, sure, it's because he doesn't —and that's not a thing I believe. You test him. You'll see. Then you'll know what his love's worth.'

He held out the notes. For one long moment Flora was looking at them, all crisp and crackly, thinking what they meant. Slowly she stretched out her hand. The deal was done.

'Angus,' said Flora that night, as the pair of them lay on the heather behind the woods of Drumgast, and the first kiss had been given. 'When are we going to get marrit?'

'Och, wuman!' he exclaimed, exasperated. 'Haff I not told you a thousand times I cannot pay for the house. You must be giving me time.'

'Angus,' she whispered, all soft and enticing, 'I haff found the money.'

He sat up abruptly. She told him all.

'But Susan iss not mine to sell!' he cried, downcast of a sudden. 'I cannot be stealing her off Drumgast.'

'It was you found her wass it not? The fawn iss no more Drumgast's than she iss yours.'

'She wass found on his property. Yon wee beast means more to Drumgast than his spaniels, and I would sooner be dead than steal a man's dog.'

Flora withdrew from his arm. 'If you think more of a roe-deer than of me, there iss nothing more to be said. I

can see now that you neffer mean to marry 'me at aal. . . .
Angus, what iss a roe-deer to a life of our own in a wee house
by the sea? It iss chust what we haff been dreaming of for
four long years. . . . So it comes to this—you do not luff
me at aal. You do not want a house, because you do not
want to marry. It iss a mistress you want. Chust that! . . .
Indeed, it will not be me!'

'I do luff you!' cried Angus, beside himself. 'I do want
to marry! It iss unchust to be saying—'

'Prove it, then! If you luff me you would not be hesitating
aal over a wee fawn. You would be leading the beast to
Mr Redebreest tomorrow at seven o'clock—not trifling
with me and making excuses. . . . Besides—Angus' (and
she slipped into his shoulder again), 'I haff taken the money.
It iss thirty five-pound notes, all crisp and crackly. We
could haff the house this very week if you saw the factor.'

'You haff *taken* the money!' gasped Angus.

'Yess, indeed—neffer wass I dreaming you would betray
me,' and she stifled her sobs. 'I wass trusting you to be true
to me.' She burst into tears.

Angus groaned. 'Cot save me from the Deffil, the
Weemen, and the Whusky!' cried he, coming nearer the
truth than ever he knew. 'So that iss the way of it? . . . Well,
yess now, indeed.'

'Give me the money,' said he at length.

'What will you do with it?'

'I will be seeing the factor in the morn, and will buy the
house on a long lease. When he has signed it, and not until,
I will be taking Susan to Cocky. . . . Cot knows what I will
be telling Drumgast.'

'Tell him she must haff been shot by poachers.'

'In her yellow collar?'

'Tell him she hass gone off to the wild wet woods and
will neffer return.'

'Aye,' said Angus. 'Indeed, aye. . . . That would be the way of it—maybe.'

All the rest of that night with Flora, Angus was silent and abstracted, and all next day on the river with Johnnie Drumgast he was thinking, 'Why should a Texan want to pay a hundred and fifty pounds for a roe-deer fawn? A hard-bargaining business man like that! Why did he go to Flora, not come to me? Some queer skullduggery iss afoot and me out of my depth already. When it iss nine o'clock I had better be as ruthless as they are.'

Cocky had the Land Rover waiting on the main road at seven. His heart was in his mouth—till he saw Angus approach with Susan in tow. A minute later he was off with her to Screavie, jubilant.

Dusk was falling over the woods of Drumgast. Sir John and Tim Tyler had finished dinner. Stretched out now before the great fire, they relished the mingled bouquet of Glenlivet and Havana. Sharp at nine as usual, that piercing whistle from Angus summoned them outside.

Cocky joined them as they passed through the hall. Tyler gave him one quick look. Cocky nodded. The almost imperceptible smile on his mouth told all that Tyler needed to know. The three of them went out to the terrace. Angus stood there all by himself. There was no food-bag in his hand. No Susan at his heel.

Sir John looked up and down the terrace. 'Where's Susan? Not like *her* to be late! . . . Gi'e her another whustle, Angus.'

'There iss no need,' declared Angus. 'It iss sorry I am to be saying it—I fear you will neffer see her again.'

Drumgast whitened. 'What has happened?'

Tyler and Cocky stood back, already, in anticipation, revelling in the lies they would now be hearing. Near to laughing though he was, Tyler composed his features.

Cocky studied the toes of his shoes.

'Man, dinna prevaricate!' cried Drumgast to Angus. 'Tell me instant!'

'Sir Chohn, I haff sold Susan.'

Tyler and Cocky started as if stung. Sir John collapsed as if pricked. 'You sold her—!' he repeated weakly.

'Sir Chohn, I wass given enough money for Susan to let me buy the house at Screavie. Four years it iss and more I haff been going with Flora of Glen Mhor, and we could not be marrit because you would not be renting the house.'

Drumgast turned purple. The veins swelled on his temples. He could find no word and Angus thought he had killed him. Then just in time he found his tongue and screamed, 'You *sold* her! Sold Susan! Hell's flaming teeth! ... You damned blackguard! Never will you set foot in that hoose. I'll fetch Niall Cameron, the polisman.'

'Sir Chohn, I haff a lease signed by your factor. I haff paid the money—three hundred pounds sterling.'

'I'll ha'e ye jailed. . . . Three hunner poonds—who paid ye that—for a fawn? I dinna believe a word. It's lees, a' lees.'

'It wass a foreign chentleman paid, though I haff promised to name no names. I know well how you feel about Susan, Sir Chohn. Sorry I am that I had to do ass I did. Wass it not me that found her? I could be finding you another, come spring. But a home for Susan iss less important to me than a home for Flora.'

'Less important to you!' Sir John choked again, but a sudden thought checked the coming explosion. . . . 'A foreign gentleman—?'

'Indeed, yess. A hundred and fifty pounds he paid, and me the rest.'

'Say,' interjected Tyler before he could stop himself, 'it was three hundred—*or was it?*' He turned a glare on Cocky.

Drumgast swivelled his eye to his guests. Hard and icy, Tyler's eye was transfixing Cocky, who stood stiff as stone, head hanging. A revealing scene it made. Drumgast saw it all in a flash. He relaxed. A frosty smile came first, and thawed to a grin. He drew a cigar from his case.

'It must vex ye sore to hear it, Mr Tyler. This Redebreest tapped ye for three hunner, but hauf went into his ane pooch. Ye've paid me the price o' an auld, near unsaleable hoose, ye owe me twa hunner bottles o' Scotch, and I'll ha'e Susan back this verra nicht, if ye dinna mind. . . . Aye, well ye ken noo—ye can tak' the word o' a Heilan' ghillie when ye canna tak' a Redebreest's.'

He had missed nothing, and gave Angus a wink as he lit his cigar. 'As for you, Angus—you've done better than ye kenned. I'll abide by the sale, and send ye a case o' Glenlivet for the wedding.'

'Redebreest,' said Tyler, and held out his hand, 'I'll be wanting the money.'

Cocky was too scared either to open his mouth or raise his head. He scurried off and came back with a wad of fifty five-pound notes. Tyler reckoned there was just one way to save his own face: to be generous. Without peeling off Redebreest's hundred, he passed the notes on to Angus. 'They were meant for you anyhow. Please accept them as my wedding present. . . . Redebreest, be off to Screavie and bring back Susan. . . . Come, Sir John, back to the fire. You can start choosing your whiskies.'

Angus married Flora in September. He used to laugh at Drumgast's notion of Highland honesty. 'It iss chust this,' said he to Flora. 'A laird iss not something a keeper's afraid of. No man lies if he's not feart, for what would be the sense of that?'

ANGUS OF THE GLENS

3

THE long Highland dusk was gathering in upper Glen Dearg. Jamie Urquhart, keeper to the Earl of Ewe, was on his way to visit his predecessor, Donald MacPherson, now in Drumgast's employ. He walked a track through heather to the white walls and red tin roof of Donald's cottage, to find him standing by the door, using the last light to knot a gut to a salmon hook.

'Och, it iss you!' cried Donald, and gave him a wide grin. 'I will be glad of your company sure enough, for it iss Chean that iss away to Glasgow to see her mother.'

He ushered Jamie indoors, for the midges were wicked.

'Donald,' asked Jamie, 'I've often wondered how you, born here and bred, who have spent aal your life as a keeper in Wester Ross, came to marry a lass from Glasgow.'

Jamie thought that Donald had not heard. The black kettle was boiling as ever on the hob and Donald made tea in silence. Through the open window Jamie could see the bats circling outside and the first star rising clear of the black hills. Donald handed him a mug and stretched his long legs to the fire.

'It iss not easy to give you the answer,' he suddenly announced. 'A delicate subchect—indeed, yess—more than you might think as an incomer. My only way is to tell you about Angus down there at Loch Screavie. Then you might be knowing why I went to Glasgow to find Chean.'

'*You* went to Glasgow!' exclaimed Jamie. Try as he might he could not fit Donald's long stride and swing from the hips into city streets. Plus-foured and booted, face tanned to the colour of peat under a faded deer-stalker, nose thin as a hawk's, brown eye as bright as a new-fallen chestnut but quickly intolerant of contradiction, Donald belonged to the moors and hills and to them only.

'Man,' laughed Donald, 'I see you think Glasgow no place to find Tonald MacPherson. But for some things Glasgow iss better than here.'

'Come, Donald! Highland lasses are the bonniest in aal the world.'

'They are as you say. I would not be denying it, for well I know it iss true. But stop you! Hear what happened to Angus MacGregor—Angus of the Glens iss what we call him now. He lived in a stone cottage by Loch Screavie, with cows and hens and five hundred head of sheep, and his father and mother too. His mother, now, the great lady she wass—she of the level gaze, the white pebble on the beach—and aye she would be looking out to Tir nan Og, and thinking on the Isles of the Blessed.

'It was Angus's chob to be herding the ewes. Well enough he did that too, when he took time off from poaching the Screavie burn. But sooner or later, every man must have a squaw. One night Angus woke up in his bed and felt he wass alone. "It iss three o'clock on a Sabbath morn," said he to himself. "I am thinking I am twenty and not yet marrit."

'Behind the croft rose the hills. Between the hills lay four passes, leading over to four glens on the far side. On that very same day Angus crossed the Bealach nam Ba to Glen Buie, where he met Fiona—she of the hair black as the raven's wing, her skin white as spring snow, and her cheeks as red as rowan-berries in September. Effery Sunday for three years he would be crossing the bealach to Glen Buie, until he and Fiona came to an understanding.

'It wass one fine evening in May, his mother sitting by the shore looking out to Tir nan Og—she of the level gaze, the white pebble on the beach—when Angus went to Murdo his father, at the lazybeds.

' "Father," said he, "I haff to tell you that for three winters and three summers I haff been crossing the Bealach nam Ba to veesit Fiona of Glen Buie."

' "Do you tell me that now, my son?" His father looked down at the long drill, and the spade, and the potatoes, and wass silent.

' "It iss the good news I haff for you," said Angus. "Fiona and I—we haff come to an understanding."

' "Iss that so, now? Well, yess, indeed." Old Murdo shook his head. He would be looking efferywhere but at Angus.

'The light died out of Angus's eye. "But father—"

' "Aye, aye, a bonny lass she iss. I wass knowing her well. You see, Angus—" Murdo cleared his throat noisily and spat from the corner of his mouth—"well it iss this, that once I wass a young lad like you, and like you I would be crossing the Bealach nam Ba to Glen Buie. There I would be meeting Fiona's mother. A bonny lass she wass too, with black hair and skin like snow, and cheeks like rowan-berries in September—chust as Fiona iss now. . . . Angus, my son—sorry I am to say it—you cannot marry Fiona, for she iss your half-sister."

'A sore hert Angus had for many a long day, I can tell you. But the time came when he woke up in his bed one night, and felt he wass alone. Said he to himself, "It iss a needful thing that effery man haff a wife. I am twenty-three and still not marrit."

27

'Next day he crossed the Bealach Beag to Glen Dorcha, where he met Morag—she of the hair red as the Cuillin at sunset, her skin like the wild bees' honey, the eyes of her green as Loch Scavaig. Effery Sunday he would be crossing the bealach to Glen Dorcha. Three years they went together, till he and Morag came to an understanding.

'It wass a misty evening in autumn, when the quick October dusk was falling, and his mother milking in the byre—she of the level gaze, the white pebble on the beach—when Angus went to his father, who wass digging potatoes at the lazybeds.

' "Father," said he, "for three winters and three summers I haff been crossing the Bealach Beag to veesit Morag of Glen Dorcha."

' "D'you tell me that, Angus?" His father looked quickly away.

' "Morag and I, we haff come to an understanding."

' "Indeed, iss that so? Well, yess, then." Old Murdo looked down at the spade and potatoes, and shook his head, and fell silent.

' "Why shake your head?" asked Angus angrily. "Why should I not marry Morag?"

' "Angus, my son, it iss a hard thing for me to say it, but, but—"

' "We haff come to an understanding," cried Angus.

' "Aye, aye. It iss a fine lass she iss—well do I know her." Old Murdo cleared his throat. "The long and short of it iss that once I wass a lad like yourself. Like you I would be crossing to Glen Dorcha. There I used to meet Morag's mother—she of the hair red as the Cuillin at sunset, the skin like honey, the eyes of her green as Loch Scavaig—chust as Morag iss now. . . . Angus, my son, you cannot marry Morag. She iss your half-sister."

'Angus went away with a hert near breaking. But the

time came when he woke up in bed one night and knew he wass alone. Said he to himself, "Above aal things, it iss needful a man haff a wife. Twenty-six I am and still not marrit. On Sunday I will be crossing the Bealach Dubh to Glen Dearg, where I will see Catriona."

'Three years he went with Catriona—she of the hair yellow as corn in August, her skin like milk that has stood in the pitcher, the eyes of her blue as the Minch in June— until they came to an understanding.

'It wass a winter evening, the air sherp, sherp, the sun standing scarlet on a black sea, and his mother scattering grain to the hens, when Angus went to his father, who wass leaning over a gate, contemplating his lazybeds.

' "Father," said he, "for three winters and three summers I haff been crossing the Bealach Dubh to see Catriona of Glen Dearg."

' "Well, now, Angus," said Murdo, "long it iss I haff wondered. . . . So, it wass Catriona." He turned away again to gaze at his lazybeds, and fell silent.

' "It iss good news I haff for you now," said Angus. "Catriona and I—we haff come to an understanding."

' "Indeed, iss that so?" Old Murdo shook his head, and cleared his throat, and looked down at the ground. "Angus, Angus, sorry I am to be telling you, but when I wass chust a lad like you I would be crossing the Bealach Dubh myself. Aye, aye, a bonny lass she wass, Catriona's mother—she of the yellow hair and skin like milk, eyes blue as the Minch— chust as Catriona iss today. . . . Angus, my son, you cannot marry Catriona. She iss your half-sister."

'Heavy wass the hert Angus had, I can tell you. But the days went by till one night he woke from a dream to find himself alone after aal. "I will burn in hell-fire," cried he to himself, "if I do not find a wife. It iss twenty-nine I am and still not marrit. Next Sunday I will be over the Bealach

Ruadh—to Flora of Glen Mhor."

'Three years he went with Flora—she of the hair brown as a roe-deer's, her skin white as foam on the ebb-tide, her eyes dark as a burn in spate. And they came to an understanding.

'It was an evening in broad summer, the air warm, warm as Flora's kiss on his lips, his mother at the beach looking to Tir nan Og, when Angus went to his father, who wass hoeing the lazybeds.

' "Father, it iss three summers and three winters I haff been going with Flora of Glen Mhor. We haff come to an understanding. We will be marrit after the sale of the ewes in September."

'Old Murdo cleared his throat and spat from the corner of his mouth. "Angus, my son, it iss me that has long been wondering—so, it wass Flora. Aye, aye. A sad thing you are telling me. When I was chust a lad like you I would be crossing the Bealach Ruadh myself. A bonny lass she wass, Flora's mother—hair brown as a roe's, skin like sea-foam, eyes dark as a burn in spate—chust as Flora iss now. . . . Angus, you cannot marry Flora. She iss your half-sister."

'It wass in black burning shame and despair, I can tell you, that Angus fled to the shore to find his mother—she of the level gaze, the white pebble on the beach, ever looking to Tir nan Og. He found her by the marram grass and cried, "Mother, Mother, I am in despair! For three years I wass going with Fiona, and three with Morag, and three with Catriona, and now three with Flora of Glen Mhor. Each time we haff come to an understanding—but each and effery time my father says, "You cannot marry, becoss they are your half-sisters." . . . It iss twenty-nine I am and still not marrit. Tell me, Mother, what am I to do, for I am in despair?"

'His mother withdrew her gaze from Tir nan Og. She

turned slowly to look at the evening star, which wass chust beginning to wink above the hills, and her eye was clear and steady.

' "My son, Angus, that iss a sad tale you haff told me. Aalways your father iss thinking he knows efferything. But stop you! This time it iss the creatt mistake he has made."

' "Mistake!" gasped Angus. "How could that be?"

' "Angus, my little one, Fiona and Morag and Catriona and Flora are not your half-sisters. You can marry whom you please, becoss you are not your father's son." '

Donald gave the fire a poke with his boot. The sparks flew upwards. 'There iss not a place,' he ended, 'but has some good to be said of it—even Glasgow.'

FHAIRSON SWORE A FEUD

4

BEHIND every platitude can lie a bitter truth, and one man who came to know it was Sandy MacTavish. 'Troubles never came singly,' he would say. His was the farm at Screavie where the moor falls from the Bealach Dubh to the Screavie burn. Poor land it was too. Many a man might have broken his heart trying to wring a living off it. On one side of him up at the bealach his ground marched with that of his laird, Johnnie Drumgast, and the other, along the burn, with that of his worst enemy, Colin Fhairson.

To the laird he owed a year's rent, and Drumgast was a hard man, a Fifer, ill to cross at the best of times, let alone owe him a year's rent. With Fhairson Sandy had a long-standing feud over the fishing rights on the river. Each swore that the other's lease gave no rights while his own did. Neither would appeal to law or laird, for the best of reasons. Many a bad word they would bellow at each other across the river beside the plank bridge.

Fhairson, called by the folk of Screavie 'Bash Fhairson,' was a great lump of a man, too ready with fist, foot, and oath. He would roar at Sandy who was lean and wiry, 'Step you across the burn, my wee man. I will bash your bones to pulp and feed them to your ploody fushes.'

'You murdering viper!' Sandy would shout, for that was his favourite cry. 'You creatt murdering viper. I will be seeing you hangit yet from the gallows.'

Who can tell but that Sandy hoped to ease his burdens when he married Flo Stotters from Mallaig. 'Troubles shared are halved,' thought Sandy, but when Flo settled in at the croft she doubled them. A bare week had passed when he found her out for what she was, a nag and a scold that never gave her man a minute's peace. He felt tormented from morn to night, what with Drumgast roaring he would put the Sheriff's officers on him, and Fhairson howling for his blood, and Flo screech-screeching at him every hour of the day. 'She iss the straw that iss breaking my back,' Sandy said to himself a week after marriage. Three months later he was saying, 'She iss not a straw but a hayrick. It iss me that iss off to Australia.'

He made all his preparations in secret. On Hallowe'en, two nights before his ship sailed from Tilbury, he slipped out of his house just as dusk was falling. His two cows were in the byre and Flo at the milking. Off he streaked across the moor and by the old bothy near the road met a tinker. Sandy was wearing his usual working clothes: a black and white check cap, a MacTavish tartan shirt, which he renewed each year on his annual visit to Inverness, and his old Harris tweed jacket and breeches. They made him easy to identify. 'When Flo finds me gone,' he thought, 'the hue and cry will be nobody's business, and the poliss will maybe search for me.'

Said he to the tinker, 'It iss a fancy dress ball at Dingwall I am off to. Here iss ten shillings if you will be changing clothes with me, so I can appear at the party as a tinker-laddie.'

The tinker eyed the tweeds and agreed fast enough. They changed in the dusk, and for good measure Sandy added his silver horse-shoe, which always he wore on a chain round his neck, and which had brought him nothing but ill-luck.

33

Then Sandy was off along the road and in no time had thumbed a lift on a fish-lorry bound for Glasgow. The tinker was stopping at the bothy, but first he went along the river to guddle a fish for his supper. Maybe it was the unlucky charm that guided his steps to the old plank bridge when Colin Fhairson was out prowling in the dark. Fhairson's eyes nearly jumped from his head when he glimpsed the check cap and tweeds of Sandy MacTavish bending over the water. Crying 'Be tamned to you!' he gave a running kick to the tinker's backside. Head first into the burn he went. 'Ye black-herted bastard of a MacTavish,' cried Fhairson, 'it iss not you that will feed on the fushes, but them on you.' Every time the tinker-man tried to climb out, Fhairson would jump on him till soon he was drowned.

Fhairson pulled out the dripping corpse and gave thought. He stripped off the clothes and laid them in a neat pile on the MacTavish side of the river. Then he hoisted the naked body on his back and sank it in the nearest bog. Lying near-by was a dead ewe, so he put that on top to keep folk away.

Oich, a right cheerful man was Bash Fhairson that night! It was not just a wee droppie of the cratur that was in him, but a draught as deep and wide as the Minch. Had the Gulf Stream been only half Talisker he would have left none to warm us all in winter. He had the end of a feud to celebrate, and the end of all bother over the fishing; besides, there were the wailings of Flo to drown—for she it was found the clothes that night. She came out to ferret her man with a lamp in one hand and her rolling-pin in the other. One moment she was yearning to hit him; the next you would have thought she liked him fine. Screech upon screech she gave, and threw her pin in the river lest she was found with it (though found it was next day in the search).

34

A good front she put on it, but any tears folk shed were for Sandy. That he had jumped in the burn to escape Flo was a thing they could understand. His found clothes were wet, but Constable Niall Cameron would well reconstruct the scene: how he jumped in the burn and climbed out quick to think again—what with the shock of water on his skin and him not used to it—how he shivered on the brink till he thought of Flo and stripped off his wet clothes to jump again. Driven out of his mind, the poor soul. The corpse had been carried into the Minch, mostlike.

Bash Fhairson continued to celebrate, drinking heavily day after day. He would not admit to himself he was afraid. The search had ended. No foul play was suspected. But Fhairson lived alone. And there, just across the dark bog, lay the corpse of a murdered MacTavish. When might it not rise? When might it not come chapping at his door? So on he kept at the 'celebrating' till a happy thought came to him: would it not be cheaper and better company by far to have a woman in the house? Besides, he could find her plenty of work, and the feeding of fowl and beast including himself. And there was Flo across the burn with no man.

Flo got along well enough for a month or two. She missed having no funeral, then as time went by she missed having no man to nag in the house, or to drive into the fold for the clipping and dipping, or to hunt into the field for drilling and sowing. And there across the burn was Colin Fhairson with no woman.

You can see how it would go. A day came when Fhairson paid her a visit, just to sense how the wind stood. Right fair it stood too. She had sore need of a bit help at the farm. In no time she was round at his place, just to see what kind of a life he was living. He had hens in the house for company and bottles on every shelf. Quickly she cleared the lot and after that there were daily comings and goings across the plank bridge.

By the end of that first year they had come to an understanding. Many and many the time Flo had to bite her tongue to keep its lash off the man, for she was not married yet. There was no proof in law that Sandy was dead. There was just the bundle of clothes, which she still kept as a kind of proof, but that was not enough.

Fhairson was nearly demented. He would have to wait years, he could see—unless the corpse came to light. Near the end of the second year he was paying the laird his rent when Drumgast remarked that he would be fishing the river Screavie next morning. 'Will you now, indeed, yess?' said Fhairson. 'I am hoping it iss the big fish you will catch.'

Great was the sensation when Drumgast's ghillie came on the corpse of Sandy MacTavish next day. Angus found it lying among the rushes at the low end of a big pool. It was screened in part by the branches of a willow, but how folk had missed it so long no one could understand. Still there it was. It was more than a little decomposed—more like a rickle of bones, no feature recognisable—still, Sandy's corpse it was for sure, because there was the silver horseshoe on a chain round its neck. Flo ran swift from the farm to identify it. 'Sandy it iss!' cried she. 'Even if there wass no silver shoe, I would be knowing him fine by the hing of his bones, the poor soul.' Genteely as you like, she buried her face in her apron and set up a wail that did her credit. 'Enough to waken the dead,' said folk, when they thought of it later.

Flo had her funeral after all. Quick it was and no flowing whisky to wind it up. Indeed, the laird never even appeared at the graveyard. He had been seeking his rent for three years now, and had in his hand the Sheriff's writ to seize Flo's stock, goods, and chattels. 'It's nae time this tae be gaein' tae funerals,' said Johnnie Drumgast to the Sheriff's officer. 'In the West Hielan's it's no' thought decent tae seize a debtor's coffin. Gi'e the widow a week tae mourn, then in ye go and aff with her coos. Tak' them early in the morn, afore she's oot o' her bed. That bitch's tongue could be more than a man would face.'

At the time of finding the tinker's corpse, a ship had been crossing the sea to England with Sandy MacTavish aboard. A different man he was now. He had been a coalminer in Western Australia and been doing well for some months, earning good money. Then as will often happen in any man's life one thing after another went wrong. First he had dysentery, and went out too soon from his bed. A cold gave him pleurisy. He lay on his bed till he thought he was better, and was newly out to the mine when a pit-prop collapsed and the roof fell on him. It broke his ribs and gashed a buttock. 'Och,' thought he, 'a week in bed will see me right.' To bed he went, and a year was to pass before he rose out of it. First the ribs gave him hell, then a long bout of rheumatic fever—or so he thought, but he was wrong. It was blood-poisoning, creeping through his weakened system from the buttock. Weeks went by before it was diagnosed. When at last they knew, they had him out to Perth by ambulance—and nearly too late. All his flesh had gone and the skin was peeling. For months he lay in chronic ill-health, at the end of all more like that tinker's rickle of bones than like Sandy MacTavish.

When the doctors had done, the worms were not missing the meal they had lost. 'Just a skeleton! Maybe Scotland is the answer,' said the doctor to Sandy. 'Go home and see if Highland air will put life in you.'

Sandy was glad to hear these words. Scotch mist and the bogs of Screavie seemed to him now like paradise, his by right, and these two years in Western Australia the wages of sin, now paid. Flo herself, at ten thousand miles, seemed not so devilish as once. A snag she was (for there's aye a snag), but Sandy was prepared to face it. He was hoping she had learnt her lesson.

He landed in England a few days after the tinker's funeral. And not unlike a tinker he felt himself. Sandy was never the man to be spending good money on clothes, but this time he was thinking he had maybe gone too far. He wore the clothes of his mining camp. Stained and thread-bare, they hung on him as loose as the shroud on a ghost—for that was what he looked most like, with his white skin, livid face, and dark eyes sunk deep in his skull, every bone of him showing.

'Och, it iss a new suit I will buy at Inverness,' said he. 'Then I will be my old self again.' But when he passed through Inverness the shops were closed for the half day, so on he went by train to Garve, then by fish-lorry to the Screavie road. Night was falling as he neared his farm. He had no wish to be seen by neighbours, coming home like a penniless tramp, so off he jumped from the lorry and took to the moor.

Threading his way through the bogs he could see a light in his window, and that cheered him—joy to his heart to be recognising every feature of ground as he came to it. There were rhododendrons, too, crouching round the grass in front, and on them some clothes that Flo had put out to air —and forgotten to take in, as always she used to do. He took a look at them. Imagine his delight when he found his old Harris jacket and breeches, and tartan shirt, and black and white check cap, the very same clothes he had given the tinker! 'Cot bless my soul!' thought Sandy. 'Flo found the poor man next day and had the very clothes off his back! It iss a hard case she iss and no mistake.'

As quick as he thought he stripped off his shabby clothes

38

and pulled on the new-aired ones. Then he stole to the window and looked in. And what should he see but Fhairson and Flo making love on his own sofa.

Keen was Flo on early marriage to counter Drumgast's threatening the law on her. She wanted Colin quick and he her. Said he to himself, 'It iss not the MacTavish will haunt ground on which Flo sets foot.' So each was agreed on a date next month, and fine was the set-to they were having, when a howl like fifty banshees came from the window. Up they started and clung to each other in mortal fear, for the cry out of the night was not canny—and there was the bony face of a dead man pressed against the glass.

They were petrified, and still more so when the door burst open and they saw the corpse of Sandy MacTavish, its great hollow eyes fiery in its white skull, dressed in the very same clothes in which it was drowned two years before. A whole week had passed since the pair of them had listened to the crumbled earth rattle on its coffin, heard the hollow thump of clods on the lid, and seen the turf replaced. Fhairson's jaw dropped, his eyes goggled. The corpse extended a long thin arm and pointed a long bony finger at Fhairson's head.

'You black-herted, murdering viper,' shouted Sandy. 'It iss to the gallows I will be hunting you.'

Flo gave scream on scream and Fhairson one squawk of blind terror. He dropped low to the floor and flashed past Sandy's legs to the door and out, shirt-tails flapping in the wind. On finding herself alone with her man's corpse, Flo gave one last screech, then fainted clean away. Sandy did his best to help her, sloshing water in her face and bosom, but each time she came round and opened her eyes, the sight of him sent her off again.

'Now, what can be wrong with you, woman?' cried Sandy in exasperation. 'You would think you wass seeing a ghost.

. . . Oich, it iss overcome with emotion she iss!' He decided to go out and bring in some neighbours, just to show the lass familiar faces and give her cause to control herself. He went a mile down the road to the village, only to find the houses empty and a ceilidh on at the village hall. So into the hall stalked Sandy. Just for one moment there was dead silence. The folk stared wide-eyed at the once familiar check cap and MacTavish tartan shirt, noting the loose, loose hang of his Harris tweeds, his bare shanks, and the sockets of his eyes, the parchment skin scarcely hiding his white bones.

A woman screamed: 'It iss the corp of Sandy MacTavish! It iss risen!' Then everyone was screaming or shouting, some rushing for the door, others smashing the windows with chairs and climbing out. Inside a minute the hall was cleared, save for Sandy and a baker's dozen of fainted women. As soon as their eyes would flutter open they would see him again, give a bit screech, and faint away. Sandy was puzzled. 'Neffer did I think they'd fail to welcome me. I haff lost weight but surely I am recognisable? It iss not murderous in the face I am like that Fhairson viper. I will haff to be trying to find out what iss troubling the folk.'

Out he went from the hall. The roads were deserted. One by one he called at the houses, but every door was barred and bolted. Patiently he would be knocking at them. Sometimes a curtain would be lifted from a window, but as quickly let fall. Though lights might blaze from the chinks, all would be silent within and no one ever answer.

At the end of his long round Sandy had just to go home to Flo—to find his own door barred too, and the shutters up on the windows. Since he could not get into the house he had to lie that night in the byre with his two cows. There was hay in a corner behind the door, and after that tiring day he slept well enough.

Long before dawn next morning the Sheriff's officer from Drumgast was crossing the Bealach Dubh to the Screavie farm. First light was spreading over the moor when he stopped by the yard gate. He noted the closed shutters. 'The auld cat will be thirled tae her bed for an hoor at least,' he muttered, and sauntered to the byre door. He pushed in the upper half and leaned his elbows over the lower. He took a good look. 'Aye, aye,' said he aloud, 'it's a braw pair o' coos the auld besom herds. They'll pay the rent owing.' At that he opened the door wide and stepped in.

Sandy had heard every word. When he saw the man prepare to make off with his cows he sprang out. 'The deffils of hell seize you!' cried he. 'Stealing a poor woman's cows while she sleeps!' He took the Sheriff's officer by the throat and made to bang his head against the wall, but the officer, at the sight of MacTavish risen, shrieked with a terror that lent him the strength of ten men. He broke from Sandy's grasp and sprang out of the byre, nor ever stopped running till he was over the hill-pass and hammering on the laird's front door.

Sandy watched the line of his flight and thought, 'He will be back with more men before nightfall. It iss Drumgast I must see or my living will be gone.' He set off at once, loping fast over the bealach to the big house. The door was open. It was the great stramash he could hear inside. He stepped into the hall and listened at the study door. Johnnie Drumgast was roasting his Sheriff's officer.

'Ye glaikit loon,' cried he. 'D'ye think me as daft as yoursel'? I dinna believe one word. That Jezebel spied ye and cam' oot. Ye were feart. The rest ye made up. Weel, back ye gang this meenute. Tak' a man wi' ye. Tak' twa. But these coos have to be in my byre this nicht.'

He had drawn breath to say more when the door of his study opened and his tongue locked in his jaw. Staring at him on the threshold stood the corpse of Sandy MacTavish. There could be no mistake. The very homeliness of that tartan shirt and diced bonnet heightened the terror of the leaden-hued cadaver. You could hear the bones rattle like castanets under the tweeds, swore the laird later. The officer gave a whinny of fear and bolted out by a back door. Drumgast sat on the edge of his chair behind his desk, his back stiff and hair on end.

'It iss a long, weary way I haff come to greet you,' said Sandy.

'Weel I ken it,' said Drumgast hastily. 'Weel I ken it, Mister MacTavish. I would no' be disturbing your weel-earned rest.'

'There hass been no rest for me where I come from, nor yet on my return. Think black burning shame on yourself, Sir Chohn Drumgast, to be seizing a poor woman's cows and me not gone two years.'

Drumgast was trembling from head to foot. 'I didna' ken, Mister MacTavish, I didna ken.'

'And what would it be you did not ken?'

'That I would be visited. . . . But I ken noo, Mister MacTavish.'

'It's often I thought I would be dead,' replied Sandy, 'before I heard a laird call me mister. It iss the first token of respect offered me since I came back. It warms the cold bones of me. I am hoping that many another time I will be able to come to you and hear a ceevil word.'

'Dinna say *that*, Mister MacTavish! Not that. There's a' your auld freends down at Screavie. I'd no' haud ye back frae their clishmaclaver. Aff ye gang, and wi' a' ma best wishes.'

' "Auld freens" did you say? It iss not them that behave like it now, I can tell you. My good neighbours aal scream and screech and show me their heels, as if they were smelling the brimstone off my bones.'

42

Drumgast leaned forward, assuming a right earnest expression. 'Be patient, Mister MacTavish. Remember they're no' used to ye. Ye've come back awfu' sudden. Gi'e them time.'

'They will be haffing plenty of that. They will be seeing me effery day, and the sooner you aal get used to me the better. . . . Happy I am to be here listening to a friendly word—but to business: I come for a reckoning.'

'Mister MacTavish,' pleaded Drumgast, 'please dinna be sae mean—'

'Mean?' cried Sandy. 'It iss you that iss the mean one, I am thinking, and me chust enchoying the roast to my choints at your open fire there. The heat wass reminding me of the place I came from. Forbye, there iss the business of the cows and the rent.'

'I didna mean to misca' ye, Mister MacTavish. I just meant, "Be generous." Try to be more generous with us short-sighted mortals.'

'Chust that! In the name of Beelzebub, what do you mean by that, man?'

'Oh, dinna be sae angry, Mister MacTavish. Dinna glower at me, I was meaning nae harm. I was meaning your ane guid. Ye'll be far happier whaur ye cam' frae. Ye said as much your ane self a meenute syne.'

'Well, indeed, it iss a kind thought you maybe haff, but little are you knowing. It iss me that likes a bit warmth, chust like yourself, and of late years I haff been used to it. But look at me! A skeleton. Hell itself I came from. Chust a skeleton I am. . . . Stop you, let me take off my shirt. You will be seeing for yourself if you do not believe me. You can be counting effery rib.'

Sandy had begun to strip off his jacket when a screech from the laird stopped him. 'Mister MacTavish, ha'e mercy on us! Ha'e mercy on me. What is it you want of me? Tell

43

me. I'll dae onything ye ask in reason, if you'll only be kind and good enough tae depart in peace.'

'Aal that I came to ask wass that you spare us the cows. The cows iss the one thing we cannot be without.'

'Dinna fret, Mister MacTavish. That gomeril o' a Sheriff's officer made a mistake. Nae haun' o' his will touch your coos again, whatever claim he may have made.'

'Well now, that iss a chentlemen's agreement. When I wass away, I made some money in the pit. In a day or two it iss me will be back and pay you this year's rent.'

Drumgast felt shiver on shiver run down his spine. 'Dae nae sic thing, Mister MacTavish. I'll no' trauchle ye wi' rent.'

'Sir Chohn! Most conseederate you haff become, and me grateful. Indeed, yess. At the November term, then, back I will come with aal the rent I haff been owing you these last three years—I will haff effery penny though I haff to pick the pocket of the Deffil himself.'

'Dinna blaspheme, Mister MacTavish! This is terrible! See ye here, it's no me that wants rent aff ye, now or ever. It's no' money I'm wanting, just peace. Dinna come again, sir. . . . I'll gi'e ye ma receipt richt noo—for your last three years' rent. Let that be the end o't. Never mention it again.'

'Overwhelmed I am by the creatt chenerosity you haff. It iss the good man you are indeed. Neffer in future will I be a trouble to you: aal the rest of my days on your ground I will be chapping on your door on term day with my rent in my hand.'

'Ma Goad, ha'e ye nae lugs, man!' exploded Drumgast. 'Will ye no tak' a telling? I've nae interest in rent. Forget it, man. I never want ye here again—I mean, I mean, whit's a wee bit rent twixt ye and me? I'd no' fash ye wi' sic a journey. . . . Mister MacTavish, I'll mak' oot the receipt tae show that ye've paid rent for a' years, past, present and future.'

44

He snatched up his pen, his hand trembling but never hesitating. MacTavish stood dumbfoundered. The pen scratched in dead silence like mice in the wainscot.

The laird read aloud: 'Received this day by me, Sir John Drumgast, from Alexander MacTavish, Esquire, and his heirs and successors, all moneys due, and all that would ever have become due in the years hereafter till the world ends, by way of rent on Screavie farm. Signed, John Drumgast.'

He pushed the paper across the desk. Sandy picked it up and read. His skull split in a happy grin. Saying to himself, 'The man's gone clean daft,' and aloud, 'It iss the noble chentleman you are, Sir Chohn,' he thrust the paper into his pocket.

'Then darken my doors no more, Mister MacTavish.'

'Satan himself will not drag me here, if that iss what you wish! Oich, it iss the good fortune that iss come on me!'

Sandy danced out of the door. He feared that all must be just a dream, or that Johnnie Drumgast would recover his senses and tear after him demanding back the receipt. He made quick time over the bealach. With this bit of paper to show to Flo he felt sure of a welcome, but when he reached his house scant welcome he got from a still-locked door and no one to answer his knock. Sorely disappointed, he went on, hoping to share his joy with whoever he'd meet. But not a soul did he meet in all Screavie. The place was deserted, like a village of the dead, though he followed the empty road right through to the far end, where the Wee Free kirk stood alone. He could hear the minister's deep voice intoning, and wondered what might be brewing in there on a mid-week morning. So in he went. Well might he wonder! The whole village was there to hear the exorcising of Alexander MacTavish's ghost.

The minister was the Reverend Doctor Michael Mac-Leod, who hailed from the Isle of Sky. Right in the middle of his exorcising, the church door opened. The sudden draught and the clatter of its closing made everyone start round, and there before them all, advancing into the body of the kirk, was Sandy MacTavish Himself.

Faster than it takes to be telling you, the kirk emptied. Folk would have died in the rush had the door not been ten feet wide. Left alone at the communion table, the minister found himself face to face with Sandy. A small sturdy man, like a black Galloway bull, he was very much the Reverend Doctor, but he had now to bolster his natural dignity. Raising arm and hand to halt the apparition, he intoned in bass: 'In the Name of Chehova, I command you—declare to me what iss the trouble of mind or speerit that brings you back to walk among us.'

'Cot bless my soul!' cried Sandy. 'Trouble has neffer been absent from me, and well you know it. In trouble I wass in my old life before I crossed over, but that wass nothing to the terrible torments that came on me out yonder. Had Old Nick been heaping the burning peats on me he could not have been doing it better. Look at me! Aye, man, it iss pity you should be feeling for me and not preaching to me of troubles.'

'Think black burning shame on you, Mister MacTavish. Many and many's the word of good counsel I spoke in your ear. Tell me this, what note did you take? But a farmer will aye be grousing when he reaps what he's sowed!'

'Oh, I mind fine what you said, meenister, and whiles I thought on it too. Och, but now there iss less need, for things iss different. I haff been changed.'

'We aal know you haff been changed, Mister MacTavish. Right sorrowful we are too, to see you in this fearful state—timely warning though it iss to my flock. Still and aal, too late it iss to be shedding tears over you, and too late for you to be wailing. . . . Come, now, be on your way, Mister

46

MacTavish. If there iss some good thing we can say or do to ease your departure, ask it.'

'Indeed, yess. Doctor MacLeod, it would ease my mind to hear why efferyone flies at the sight of me—saving Chohnnie Drumgast and he iss now out of his mind. I may changed—still, I am at heart the same old Sandy Mac-Tavish.'

'Mister MacTavish, man iss made aalways to be seeking his safety. It iss not yourself should expect different, now that you know what awaits. No man can feel fraternal with the likes of you, even for a space—unless he can rise above nature, like an anchel, or a meenister of the Free Kirk.'

'It iss that Fhairson that hass been spreading tales about me! The murdering viper that he iss! I will—'

'Silence!' thundered the Reverend Michael. 'Be not forgetful that you stand in the House of Chehova! Blame no one but yourself. There iss no man, woman, or child of Screavie could be at ease in your presence. Begone, sir! Back to where you came from.'

'Stop you! I haff come to Screavie to stay. Neffer again will I leave. Och, my neighbours will haff to get used to seeing me in my old haunts.'

'It iss joking you are,' gasped the minister. 'You cannot be serious? It iss not possible!'

'Not choking but choyful. Rent free I will be foreffer and a day.'

The minister shuddered, despite himself. 'Mister MacTavish!' he shouted. 'You must not be doing this to us. The time is come for you to be off back to the Pit, where you belong. Away with you! Stand not upon the order of your going, but go.'

'Iss that not a mean, unchenerous thing for a meenister of the Free Kirk to wish a poor deffil!'

'Man, you haff confessed it wass your due.'

47

'Maybe so. But I haff escaped and will neffer go back.'

'When it iss tamned you are it iss tamned foreffer. There iss no second chance for you, Mister MacTavish, so get you gone. If it iss not to the Pit you will go, then be off to the far ends of the earth.'

'Chust that! Me that should be your prodigal son, banished! It iss easy said. But you cannot take the trews off a Highland chentleman. I haff not money for so long a chourney.'

'Now, now, none of your vapours. Go by the line you came.'

'I came by the P. and O. shipping line. The mining company paid the fare from Australia, not me.'

'The P. and O.—Australia—it iss a joke you are telling me!' The minister stretched out a tentative hand and poked MacTavish in the ribs. 'Cot bless my soul! Sandy MacTavish himself, the black-herted villain that he iss! Not the Infernal Mister MacTavish at aal!'

He seized Sandy by the hand and ran him out of the kirk. 'It iss to Flo we must go,' cried he, 'and tell her you are mortal man before she does herself an inchury. Her eye hass been crazed since she saw you walk in last night.'

As they hurried through the village street all doors were shut tight and many an eye peeked from behind the blinds and curtains, and many a head was shaken. A strange sight it was to see the pair of them, cackling together as if they were geese, yet hurrying on as if some frightful fiend trod close behind. It was said the minister had recanted his faith and thrown in his lot with the devil.

Sandy told the minister all that had happened these last two years, and the Reverend Michael told what the folk of Screavie had believed. When they came to the farmhouse the minister shouted through the locked door, 'Flo, Flo, your man iss alive! He was neffer dead. I haff him here.'

Flo heard but would not open the door or shutter, nor believe a word said, then or after. Next morning she was off to her mother at Mallaig and never came back.

A happy man was Sandy, all troubles gone—rent paid forever, Flo flown, and Fhairson in the hands of the law—for such a fright had he taken that night that he had run all the way to Constable Niall Cameron at the police station and confessed to the murder. On the day Fhairson was hanged, Sandy took a holiday in Inverness. He bought a new diced bonnet, a MacTavish tartan shirt, and a silver medal on a chain showing the Archangel Michael spearing a devil.

MARCH HARE

5

NEVER had the men of Ross known such a wild March. Big winds followed thick blizzards. Cars, trucks, and buses stuck for two days and nights on Scotland's backbone at Strath Bran and the Dirrie More while fast-drifting snow routed the snow-ploughs. A brief thaw released them, but it came with torrential rain and hail, followed suddenly by days of black frost. The mountains of Wester Ross had never looked more Alpine, sheeted as they were in sparkling ice, when down rolled cloud, dark and thunderous, soon to be white with lightning. This new storm heralded day upon day of snowfall, declining into a short thaw till the frost renewed itself—and this time it was to hold for six weeks.

On his way home from Switzerland, Simon, the Earl of Ewe, arrived at Screavie Inn to find the very conditions of which a skier dreams on wet winter nights. The mountains were plastered. Their crowded tusks pillared a sky of deep unsullied blue. The thermometer outside the inn registered forty degrees of frost, and indoors the beer had burst the bottles.

His wife Shuna was not due back to join him till noon tomorrow. Hearing from Meg Chisholm, the innkeeper, that the first car in a month had won up Glen Dearg today, he hastened after it, hoping to spend a few hours with his former keeper, Donald MacPherson. Donald lived with his wife Jean in a cottage below Sgurr Dubh. Simon greatly wondered how they had fared—ill, he suspected. Cut off from supplies for weeks, they must be starving. He drove benevolently up the narrow glen, feeling like Santa Claus with a sackful of tins and bread.

His reception bewildered him. 'Well, iss it not yourself!' exclaimed Donald joyfully. 'Man, I am glad to be seeing another belly to fill.'

Sarcasm was foreign to MacPherson. Simon felt a sudden loss of understanding. 'Don't you worry, Donald, I've brought lots of food.'

'Well now, that would be the last thing we need here,' said he. 'It iss more mouths we want to eat aal the meat.'

Simon's whisky was welcome if not his tins, and they sat by the fire while Jean dropped scones on the girdle. Simon had to press him. 'Have you ever seen the like of these four weeks?' he asked, falling into Donald's idiom, which was so infectious. 'And you not able to get out of the glen. Had you seen it coming, and laid in food?'

'No' him!' cried Jean, more than a hint of exasperation in her voice. 'He's west heilan' an' feckless. When they blizzards cam' doon there was hardly a bite in the hoose, an' himself in bed with a chill in the stomick.'

Donald gave Simon a wink. 'Yess, indeed, coming ass she does from Glasgow she does not haff the trust in Providence we haff learnt in Ross.'

'Wheesht man, had it no' been for my hens and my bag of flour, we'd be starving the day.'

Donald's eye narrowed. 'Iss that so, indeed! Look you!'— and he suddenly glanced up at a pair of old antlers secured by two nails to the wall over the fireplace. Simon followed his eye and saw hanging from one of the points a piece of red flannel.

'There iss your answer, woman—(to Simon) in yon piece

51

of red stuff, for that is aal you will be thinking it iss.'

As if regretting this outburst, he looked at the toe of his boot, and he looked at the fire, but he would not look Simon in the eye. Jean had turned suddenly to hide her face too.

'Tell me what happened,' commanded Simon.

'I do not like to,' he confessed. 'For you will not be believing me when you hear.'

'Donald!' expostulated Simon. 'Never yet have I had cause to doubt a word of yours.'

'Well, then. That iss kind of you to say so—though true it iss too—yess. It iss true. Well then . . . Yess.'

'C'mon, Donald.'

'Man, that wass the terrible snowfall we had. A whole series of storms. Snow driving so fast we could not see across the burn and me in my bed with my stomick while poor Chean there had to be dig-digging at the door to clear it each morning. Then it wass wind, wind, wind—biting and icy with the drifts deepening on the road till no man could get in or out. We had only flour and tea left in the house and no meat to keep the cold from our bones. We wass desperate. After thunder and flood came the frost. I wass so desperate I climbed out of my bed.

' "Chean," said I, "I will be climbing up to the bealach between Sgurr Dubh and Sgurr Ban. It may be the Lord will send me a wee beast to shoot."

'I took both my gun and my rifle. Who could be telling what I should find? That terrible cycle of weathers had not been canny. I could be sure of nothing. What I might see could be strange.

'The sun was chust up when I came on the road, for well I knew the day would be long whereffer I went. Sure enough, as soon as I stepped off the road I wass knee-deep, and so it wass aal the way up the Allt Dubh. The sun was high before

52

the slope eased off towards the bealach, and the hills shining. It wass my eyes that were paining me, I can tell you. All this while not a living thing stirred, neither close at hand nor far off, save my own breath on the air. Nothing but a shining whiteness. Man, if you could haff seen Sgurr Dubh you would haff liked her fine. She was machestic.

'Well, then. I wass on the last slope to the bealach when I saw something move. And when I looked, there wass the ears of a white hare against the blue sky. So I crept up with my gun till I could be sure of her. When I fired—the wee besom skipped off out of sight! Neffer haff I missed a hare at that range. I should haff cried had I not been so angry. . . . I crept up again—and there she wass still. This time I saw the whole of her—and there wass something red about her middle. But I did not stop to think about that. At forty paces I fired—and away she skipped. I could not believe it. Neffer, neffer could I miss at forty paces. She had bounded chust a few steps, and there she sat with her long ears, washing her whiskers mark you, cheeky as you like. It wass me felt a fool, I can tell you . . . I crept up to thirty paces. I wass sure of her now and fired. But away she bounded, chust a few steps, and sat washing her whiskers, watching me aal the while out of the corner of an eye.

'It wass then I knew she wass not an ordinary white hare. There wass thiss red thing at her middle and I would be wasting effery cartridge I had on her. But stop you! My father had been a keeper in Torridon and his father too, and I knew what to do. I opened a cartridge with my knife and popped in a silver sixpence. Then I loaded my gun. I took aim. I fired. And she fell dead.

'When I picked her up by the ears, what would you think I found? . . . Man, she wass wearing a red waistcoat. When I looked in the pocket, there wass my silver sixpence. . . . Look you! There iss the waistcoat above the mantel.

53

You will see the sixpence in the pocket too, if you will haff the patience to wait till I finish.

'Well, then, yess. That wass chust a hare.

'On I went to the bealach, wondering what I should do next. When I looked down on the other side to the head-waters of the Allt Ban, what should I see but a herd of deer, stags and hinds together, huddled on the floor of the upper corrie. The wind was south-east, so I climbed on to Sgurr Ban to come to their westward, where they could not scent me. High above them now, I traversed out across the flank of the corrie. I started down to them. They were at rest straight below.

'Before long the snow wass balling on the heels of my boots. I stopped to kick them free. A piece of the hard snow began to roll. It became a ball and rolled more and grew bigger. Soon it wass off hell-for-leather down the slope. In a moment it will break, I thought. Aalways they break. But this one did not break. Even when chumping in the air, aalways it landed on deep soft snow and rolled on. It grew chigantic. I watched it go right down to the floor of the corrie. Still it held together. I groaned, 'It will be scaring the deer!' It flashed right into the middle of them and they vanished.

'It wass my hert that wass broken, I can tell you. I thought to traverse back to the bealach, only the snowball wass so big that I felt I must go down to see it, perhaps measure it too, so that I could tell Chean. When I came close-to, glad I wass I had come. Neffer had I thought a ball of snow could be so big—as big as Screavie Inn. I began to pace it out chust to prove it. As I went round a strange sight met my eye. Something wass sticking out of the ball. When I looked I saw it wass a hoof. Farther on wass an antler, then a foreleg, then a tail.

'When I broke open that snow-ball I found inside it ten

54

stags and fourteen hinds and ninety-nine hares. Neffer haff we had so much meat in the house. Chust you ask Chean. If you do not believe me, she will be telling you.'

'Ninety-nine hares!' Simon boggled. 'Tell me, Donald, why did you not make it one hundred hares?'

Donald's face flushed with indignation. He sat up straight. 'Cot bless my soul!' he swore, 'I would not be making myself a liar for the sake of one hare!'

THE DEVIL'S CAVALRY

6

SHUNA, the Countess of Ewe, stood by the great pool on the Allt Dearg near Screavie and watched Donald Mac-Pherson cast his fly. The water came strong and brown through a long rock gut, then broadened to a pool one hundred yards long and deeper than eye could fathom. The banks were of red Torridon sandstone and the salmon lying in tile under the overhangs. Save for the gentle, barely perceptible stir of their tails, they were motionless. She watched spellbound at the delicate precision of each cast, the fly alighting as if by sheer accident of flight. But no fish moved.

Suddenly, Donald wound in his reel. 'It iss not them that will feed this day, nor we on them. For sheer capriciousness, only a Chinese camel can beat a salmon.'

'It iss the sad look you have on your face, Donald,' she answered, and passed him her whisky flask.

When he had set it down a while later, she asked, 'Donald, I heard that you once worked in China. What kind of job took you there?'

'There iss but one kind of chob I would know, and that is the keepering.'

'In China?'

'Indeed. Or it could be said I wass a herdsman. It was a mixture of the two I wass.' The nostrils of his nose distended as he tried to recall details and to set the facts in order.

'It all began when I wass a young ghillie on the old Earl of Ewe's forest. In these days he had the ground on both sides of Loch Screavie and wass the worst kind of master you could haff—an absentee landowner. He had been made Ambassador at Peking when one spring day Ninian Campbell the factor came chapping at my door with a long telegram in his hand. "It iss you that iss off to China," said he, "and you must be on a plane this week."

'It was little he would tell me, the blaggard, for well he knew I would not haff gone had I known. I wass chust twenty-two years, and Campbell picked me out from aal the ghillies ass the man who could best be spared. I wass to teach the Chinese my trade, said he with a smirk, and it wass me that wass believing him. You will be noting,' added Donald a thought defensively, 'that here wass a time when I wass not only young but innocent too.

'Well then, there I wass at Peking chust ten days later, with a car and a secretary to meet me at the airport as if I wass the Earl himself. He rushed me off to the embassy and before I knew wass leading me into a cocktail party—chust like a fankful of sheep, so creatt wass the press—until the Earl himself stood before me. Red ass a cherry he wass behind creatt white whiskers. I did my best to put him at his ease, the poor man, for sore harassed he must haff felt with aal those folk about him. "Well now," says I to him, "had your lordship been telling me it wass as hot as this, it iss a bottle of Highland air I would haff brought as a present."

'But never a smile came on his lordship's face. He wass looking me up and down, up and down. . . . Aye, true it iss, I wass wearing my tweed chacket and plus-fours and my hill boots, for it wass a bothy or lodge I thought to veesit,

57

not an embassy. It wass then I saw that the Earl wass not a chentleman, though not a word had he said. A chentleman will neffer be vexing you unless he means to.

' "God bless my soul," said he (Donald perfectly mimicked a southern England accent), "are you not a bit young, MacPherson?"

' "Not I," said I, "if it iss work on hill or moor you need of me, and not as a diplomaniac."

'He wass looking me up and down again from collar to boots. "You have no other suit?" he asked.

' "Indeed, I haff that," said I, "but this iss not the Sabbath."

'He spoke sudden-like to his secretary, "Bring me Anton Solovensky." Then, turning to me, "He's a Russian scientist. Ranks high in his own country. He asked me for help in running an expedition to Outer Mongolia. Unexpected emergency. He would like a Scotsman to discipline drovers and pack-animals. In a rash moment I said I had the very men for such work on my Ross-shire estate. I had thought of an older man. You're too young, MacPherson. Campbell should have sent an older man. But we'll have to leave that to Solovensky."

' "You will haff to leave it to me too," I said. "I will not be going to Outer Mongolia with a ploody Russian."

'At that very moment a man stepped to my elbow. He bowed to the Earl and signed him to leave us together. He said to me (here Donald mimicked a deep and plummy Russian accent), "My name is Anton Solovensky. What is your name, please?"

'It wass a good look I took at him. He wass a wee man like a Pict. His face was broad, broad, but lean too and pale as his linen suit. A soup-strainer moustache hid the mouth but the eyes of him were bright and brown and restless. Black hair stood up on his head like a hayrick.

' "Donald MacPherson iss my name," said I. "And what would you be wanting of me?"

' "Donald—MacPherson...." He rolled the words round his tongue as if it wass Talisker. "It is good to be hearing a Scottish accent again. At Hogmanay you will be reciting *Tam o' Shanter* to me."

' "Man!" I exclaimed. "Neffer did I think a Russian could tell a Scot from an Englishman."

' "From a Sassenach," he corrected. "A bloody Sassenach." He snapped his fingers. "Ha! Always you think us parochial, like your Cockneys. We know more than you think. Did you know that I, as a young man, go to Glasgow? There I study engineering." He seized my arm. "Let us go —let us take a walk. I want to speak to you. Zere is something I want to ask."

'Glad I wass too of the chance to get away. He told me his tale while we walked down Ha-ta-men street.

'He wass off to explore the Gobi Desert itself, and creatt wass the expedition he planned. But so proud wass he of himself he could hardly speak at first for puffing out his chest. "This," he declaimed, "is the world's biggest expedition. You English!" he exploded (forgetting me): "You fritter your time trying to climb ze Mount Everest. A mountain! Of what use is a mountain? MY expedition will be quite different—it will be ze vastest expedition to cross ze Gobi since Jenghiz Khan! I shall be away two, three years and more. I shall carry vast stores food, vast equipment. I shall need 'oondreds an' 'oondreds an' 'oondreds of camels. Zat is why I come here. Ze government give me special permission. I hire vast camel stock in East China.

' "Ah, but zese camels! Zey are to Anton Solovensky a personal and peculiar headache—ze Devil's Own Cavalry. Zey are even now being herded at Changpeh, about one 'oondred and fifty miles to our west beyond ze Great Wall.

My supplies are zere too, waiting to be sorted into loads.

' "I need help," he continued. "I am being driven mad by camels! Always zey cause trouble. Zey go fight, breed, fall sick, run away. My nineteen Russian comrades, zey are from ze army and universities, to be freed only at ze last moment. I need an overseer at Changpeh. I need him to rule ze camel-drovers, to engage and pay coolies, to weigh, watch, guard zese precious loads. I need him now. I have only two comrades zere. Do you know, we have loads and loads of gold and silver coin in crates to pay our coolie-wages and to buy food and fodder in ze villages, and to hire pack animals if any camels fall by ze wayside? I am *des*perate! Are you willing to help?"

'It wass a wary man I felt, I can tell you. "Well, yess, indeed," said I. "Sheep and cattle and red deer are not camels. It will be different habits they haff, I am thinking, and me not knowing them." Quick I had to be in deciding. Aalways a man will be wanting to go on an expedition, chust to see. Who could be telling but this might be my only chance in a lifetime. So I stamped down my caution. "True it iss," I said, "they are aal four-legged beasts to be sure. If I can herd and drive the one, so I can the other. Now, what pay will you be giving me?"

' "Pay!" he exploded. "Zere is no pay!" He stopped in the street, overcome at the notion. He turned on me in wrath. Emphasising each point with a forefinger-dig in the chest, he almost shouted, "I shall feed you, I shall house you, I shall clothe you—zen take you on my great expedition too!" Suddenly he threw out his arms: "We shall explore all ze Gobi. We shall travel westward to ze spurs of ze Altai mountains, an' see wonderful zings, and endure glorious hardships. An' I will come back famous as your Christopher Columbus—I will be given ze Order of Lenin.... Yet none of zis will cost you a rouble, my friend. Do not speak to me of pay! A true Scotsman you are, my braw, canny hielan' man! It is to ze unknown I lead you. . . . Tell me, now, what do you say?"

'My mind was made up. I looked Solovensky straight in the eyes: bold and ruthless under shaggy brows, they shone like a Wee Free preacher's when he waxes fanatical. Aye, he wass a dreamer, wass Solovensky, but his real dreams were of himself and not of his science.

' "I will be coming," I said. "When do we start?"

' "Ze end of zis month. But we go too fast: you say you do not know camels. Can you manage a vast—a what you say?—a *multitude* of camel?"

'It wass now or neffer. Also it was spring. I drew my breath and plunged. "Leave you the camels to me!"

' "Excellent! It is settled then! Tomorrow morning you come with me to Changpeh, beyond ze Great Wall."

'I nodded. I had choined the Russian expedition to the Gobi Desert.

'Neffer haff I worked so hard as in these three weeks that followed. My chob was to supervise both camels and camel coolies. Neffer can there haff been such a congregation of camels since the break-up of the Imperial Camel Corps. They were herded in a creatt stockade outside the town, at the edge of the seasonal road running north-west to Outer Mongolia. My chob wass the feeding of the beasts, and the payment and drilling of several hundred coolies who tended them. Thus I freed the Russians to look after their own stores.

'The month drew to its close. The Russian party gathered —twenty men all told. This reinforcement wass the solving of aal problems save mine. No one knew a thing about camels. Yess, indeed, these scientific ghillies would be telling me aal about the natural history of the *Camellus bactrianus*: but deffil a one would come within biting range. I had to wrestle with my fate alone, and much troubled in

61

soul I wass growing—the more so by my very success.

'You will be laughing at me when you hear it, but I had won a creatt reputation ass a camel man. By virtue of chust three weeks' hunting of camel coolies I wass thought an expert in camels. Day by day, Solovensky wass becoming so lofty and patronising that neffer would I confess the truth— the truth that I knew nothing, for I only manached the men who manached the camels. Each day more camels were coming. Effery day camels were falling sick, stampeding, refusing their food, fighting or mating or giffing birth. So long as we stayed at dead stop at Changpeh, we could manache them. The individual problems they put could be answered by the one or two drovers who knew what to do. But each day that passed made me more uneasy of the future. It wass Chief Transport Officer they were calling me now. The idea of a big-scale operation, the thought even of a move, wass appalling me. At last I went to Solovensky—the "Kommissar" they called him.

' "Sir," I said (for I wass no Comrade), "I am feeling no confidence in these camels of yours."

' "MY camels, did you say?" exclaimed Solovensky. He sucked in his lean cheeks and squinted down into his walrus whiskers. "My dear MacPherson, consider them yours! You must have confidence in your camels. *I* have confidence in *you*."

' "Listen," said I. "It iss the *camels* that haff to carry your loads."

' "Stop being timid! You irritate me. You must learn to obey my orders at once. You must jump to them. . . . Now, MacPherson, you have been father and mother to your camels. They will obey every word you say. Even the drovers speak well of you!—and they are worse than camels. You deal fair—they burst with gratitude!"

' "Stop you," said I. "No *camel* effer was grateful.

Camels are aal right asleep or at gress. But the moment we say "Go," Cot alone knows what will be happening. There are too many. It iss a rehearsal I will be needing."

' "All right, all right. We shall have a rehearsal. We shall rehearse a loading and unloading. Will that satisfy you? Come, let us look at your loading plan. We'll make a check, then rehearse on the day after tomorrow. On the third day— we are off!"

'It was agreed.

'On the day of the dress rehearsal, I had aal my coolies out at dawn. By nine o'clock, seven hundred and fifty loads had been laid out in rows on the plain before the stockade. Four hundred coolies stood in ranks ten deep beside them. Then Kommissar Solovensky drove up with his nineteen comrades—but no longer wass he chust a Kommissar. Like Chenghis Khan himself, ringed by his Cheneral Staff, he came to review his cavalry. He walked in slow step down the broad passage between the men and the massed loads, then took his station at the top of a hill, from which he looked down on the parade ground.

'At this I blew my whistle. The army of coolies broke rank and ran towards the stockade. They hurled aside the tree-trunk barriers and led out the camels, each beast to its load.

'They made a vast host. They filled the plain: camels from Antung and Shantung, from Wopeh and Shansi, camels from Korea, camels without end. In a word, eight hundred camels. It was the smell of them and their snuffling and dust and dung that wass pervading aal China, I can tell you. At the very centre were the fastest camels of aal, fifty camels from Korea. It wass me had chosen them too, strong in the leg and lively, to carry the cargo of most value —the expedition's treasure-chest. Four hundred bags of gold and silver coin were there, worth forty thousand pounds.

63

'Creatt wass the fear I had lest the loading and unloading of so many beasts run away with aal daylight hours, leaving us no time to march, so that we should be at Changpeh foreffer—chust loading and unloading. But inside two hours the chob wass done. Indeed, it wass the choyful man I wass. Here were eight hundred camels, loaded by eleven o'clock! Arrayed in trim lines, waiting.

'I went to Cheneral Solovensky and reported. So puffed up he wass that he stood like Chehova. Creatt wass the effort he had to make, I can tell you, chust to bring his head down from the clouds and give a bit credit where it wass due.

' "Hear again what I always said," he cried. "Camels can tell a Scotsman. 'Here is a hard case,' they grunt, 'let us not push him too far.'" He paused, as if to search his mind for another compliment, but not one could he find, for aal his thoughts dwelt on that Deffil's horde. He looked down upon the plain below:

' "They are like the cavalry of Jenghiz Khan," he cried, and waved his Imperial arm. "They stretch to the rim of Asia, they strain forward, eager for the march, Invincible, Servants of Karl Marx, of Lenin, of our Party Leader—"

'These camels heard him. Even as we watched, and his pride mounted, a high-pitched squeal rang out from the centre of the host. Well I knew that squeal: an angry Korean camel had bitten the tail of the camel in front. The victim snapped at the first tail to his own nose. Another squeal! And another! Squeals abounding. In a trice, a knot of Korean camels were biting right and left at centre. Looking down from above, we could see that knot of disorder swirl and spread. A meenute later it happened—aal the eight hundred beasts stampeded. The coolies—but as well might flotsam stop a tidal wave. A yellow fog rose up and obscured the plain, and from the hert of it rose a drumming like thunder.

'But hear you this. When the Bactrian camel stampedes, it goes home. The camels from Outer Mongolia went back to Outer Mongolia. The camels from Manchuria and from Antung and Shantung, and from Wopeh and Shansi, and those decadent, imperialistic camels from Korea (with the gold and silver coin), aal broke for home at a mad gallop. The dust of their hooves mounted up to the sky. And when at long last the dust-screen was settled, not a camel wass there in sight. No, nor a coolie either—they had fled from the wrath to come.

'Up there on the hill stood Cheneral Solovensky, surrounded by the nineteen men of his Imperial Staff, and me, Tonald MacPherson. Dull-eyed and speechless, aal of us stared at the empty plain. There wass no point even in wishing the camels back. Long before they could be rounded up their loads would be looted. Not a thing would be left. We aal knew it. We were speechless. There wass nothing to be said—yet a creatt need to be saying it. I turned to Solovensky, him a cheneral no more, in whose eyes these camels had been my camels.

' "What do we do now?" I asked him.

'For a few terrible seconds I wass fearing he would burst, so red had his face become. Then he swung upon me. His hands smote together behind his back, and his chin stuck out.

' "I give you my last order," he snapped. "Do what your camels have done. Take the short route to your own country."

'Of aal the orders he effer gave me, that wass the one I obeyed quickest. It wass on my tongue to be telling him the ploody camels were his, not mine. But I did not stay long enough: forbye, it wass trouble enough he had without putting blame on himself.'

BLACK ERCHIE
7

ARCHIE MACFARLANE was the fisherman at Screavie, the only one the village had, for although it lay at the head of a sea-loch there was no pier or port, save for a jetty or two. Ullapool and Gairloch were the ports for the fishing fleets. Archie was born at Ullapool and bred to the sea and boats. He fished with the fleet till his mid-twenties, 'But aye he wass a rebel,' said folk afterwards. Soon he would own no master but himself. So down he came to Loch Screavie, rented an old croft-house on the north shore off Johnnie Drumgast, and set up as village fisherman. 'Black Erchie' they called him, from his hair and eyes.

True it is, he could have been earning better money at Ullapool, 'But och,' he said, 'I do well enough. It iss not money I want, it iss chust to be left alone to go my own way.' There were fish in the loch to give him a living. He sold his catch locally, and at villages up and down the coast, where fish were always hard to come by unless a man caught them himself: the fleets send theirs off by lorry to Aberdeen and England. Erchie filled a need.

One night in September, Erchie was having a dram by his fireside to celebrate his thirty-sixth birthday. He was unmarried, but his son Dougal was there too, having come for the night from Cairnban at the mouth of Loch Screavie, where he ran a ferry boat. Here they were, then, just settling

66

down for a night on the whisky, and a song or two with Drumgast's and Ewe's ghillies, who were coming in later, when a knock came on the door.

'Come in!' shouted Erchie.

The door was opened by a young woman, maybe of twenty-eight years. It was she of the hair yellow as corn in August, with skin like milk that has stood in the pitcher, and the eyes of her blue as the Minch in June.

'Cot bless my soul!' cried Erchie. 'Come right in and let us look at you. . . . Tell me who would you be?'

'Och, father,' said Dougal, 'it iss Catriona of Glen Dearg, from over the hills.' He rose at once and poured her a cup of tea.

'I am not in Glen Dearg now,' she said. 'I haff newly taken service with old Chacob Frewin at Screavie House. It iss house-keeper I am with a lass in the kitchen.'

'Do you tell me that, Catriona? Will it be salmon he iss wanting?' asked Erchie, 'or white fish or lobster?' He had been supplying Screavie House for more than ten years.

'It iss Erchie MacFarlane he wants, not fush,' said Catriona. 'He hass sent me to ask you to come at once.'

'Och, I cannot do that. Old Chacob iss turning ninety, and still as daft as effer he was. What iss it he wants now? Today iss my birthday and the ghillies coming in. You be telling old Chacob I will be coming tomorrow.'

'Stop you! He iss making his last wull and testament,' said Catriona. 'A lot he has talked of Erchie MacFarlane these last few days, and even asked my opeenion. When I said we were not acquainted, says he in reply, "Good! No news is good news," whateffer he meant by that. He iss ailing, Mr MacFarlane. There hass been a creatt coming and going of doctors and specialists, and he says himself he has not long to live. I would not be knowing what he wants of you. My advice iss, come.'

'Catriona iss right,' urged Dougal. 'He might leave you a hundred pounds, and you wanting new nets. The night's young. I'll be here to let in veesitors.'

Erchie rose without another word and began pulling on his sea-boots. 'How did you come, lass?'

'I walked round the head of the loch.'

'I will be taking the boat. Less than a mile straight across.'

Screavie House stood on the farther shore, directly opposite Erchie's cottage. Old Jacob Frewin had been there twenty years. He was grand-uncle to the new Earl of Ewe. When he had retired from his shipping company he had wanted to live near the sea. The old Earl had been quick to sell him Screavie House, in the hope he would look after young Simon and leave his money in the family, for Jacob had never married. He was eccentric: never could anyone tell what he would be up to next. In his old age he had taken to religion—he who had not set foot in a kirk for half a century. He sat in his pew every Sabbath morning these last ten years, but never yet was seen to put money in the plate. He kept an account of each sermon by date and text, and marked down its worth in the margin—sometimes five pounds, more often one or less down to tuppence. At the end of each year he would send the account to the Reverend Doctor Michael MacLeod with his cheque for the lot.

It was a dark night and rough on the water, but the lights of Screavie House beckoned them on. When Catriona led Erchie into old Jacob's bedroom he was sitting propped up on the pillows, looking very much alive: there was red in his cheeks and a shine on the white hair.

'I'll not keep you long,' said he. 'My time has come and my will is to make. Simon along at the castle is hoping my siller's for him and his. I've another mind. He's a spend-thrift and his wife like him.'

68

'I hear that iss all changed,' counselled Erchie, 'now that he and his lady are friends.'

'I cannot abide women,' rasped Jacob: 'Satan's progeny for the ruination of man and man's best works. You should know it, Archie.'

'Aye, sir, sore they are to thole, with their tempers and tantrums and lack of reason. Still and aal, I would as soon be dead as without them.'

'You still think you would? I've made inquiries about you, Archie. Your son Dougal is a bastard off an Ullapool woman, who fairly turned the tables on you by running off south—leaving the bairn on your doorstep.'

'Och, I wass chust eighteen then—the same as Tougal iss now.'

'You were needing the lesson. I hope you learnt it well. You've never married since—that pleases me. You're over fond of whisky, but I see the reason for it. You've never been inside the kirk, but I know the way to mend that. You earn your living off the sea, and so did I. In short, you're a rebel as I was. I intend to make you my heir, if you're willing.'

'Cot bless my soul!' exclaimed Erchie. 'I am not deserving that! I am not your kin.'

'You're more akin to me than my grand-nephew is. I didn't fetch you here to tell me what to do, but to answer a plain question. Will you take my property if I leave it you?'

'I don't mind if I do,' said Erchie. 'How much is it?'

'The total estate is worth four hundred thousand pounds. I have it placed out of reach of death duties.'

Erchie blinked. 'It should see me out my time.' Otherwise he was speechless.

'It will. In the first fifteen years you'll receive interest only—about ten thousand pounds a year, less tax. Thereafter you'll get an outright gift of the capital sum. But all this will happen only if you obey certain conditions. These conditions will vex you at first, and seem hard. Later you'll grow used to them, be schooled by them, and come to thank me for them as serving your own good. I brought you here tonight to hear them. Turn them down if you will. Listen first. Sleep on them tonight. Then come here at midday tomorrow and say to me yea or nay.'

'So that iss it!' exclaimed Erchie. 'I wass thinking it wass too good to be true. . . . Let me be hearing the worst.'

'The first condition is this. Every day after my death you must come to my grave in Screavie kirkyard at any time before noon, and there say a prayer for the rest of my soul and the enlightenment of your own. Only two excuses for any omission will be accepted: the first for illness, which must be attested by a medical certificate, sent within one week to the minister or to the Earl of Ewe; the second for thirty consecutive days' holiday each year, which may be taken at any time you wish.

'The second condition is that you must not marry. If you fail in either of these two conditions, then one-tenth of my property goes to the kirk and the rest to the Earl of Ewe. That is all.'

'All!' exclaimed Erchie. 'Chust that! My life would become a fair misery.'

'With four hundred thousand at your back?'

'Och, the money iss no use if I am to be caged.'

'Are you caged now? In what way would your life be different? A visit to the kirkyard for a couple of minutes each day: that would be all the difference. Suppose you had my money all at once to spend in the capital cities: it would ruin you. The evil traits would develop and eat you up: more women like the Ullapool girl, more bastards like Dougal. You would be upsides Drumgast as a whisky connoisseur. At Screavie you get blind only at Hogmanay,

St Andrew's Night, and the Burns Supper. As for the lasses here, they are well able to look after themselves. Am I not right, Catriona?'

Catriona had been standing well back near the door. 'Aye, sir,' she said. 'They haff to be smert at Loch Screavie.'

'Then what advice would you give to Archie?'

'I would say that if he iss as wise as you he will take the money.'

'There you are,' concluded Jacob. 'Go away and think it over. Show Mr MacFarlane out, Catriona. Good night to you.'

A bewildered man was Erchie as he stumbled down the stairs and out. At the front door he stopped. 'What should I be doing, Catriona?' he pleaded. 'It iss a terrible position I am in to be sure. It iss not me that knows what to think.'

Catriona blushed with pleasure at this mark of respect. 'I would not be daring to advise a chentleman,' she answered. 'I am chust old Chacob's servant.'

'Why, you advised me when he asked upstairs, Catriona. What would you say when he iss not hearing you?'

She looked at Erchie, at his black thick hair and bold eye, and his strong, weather-beaten face, and the poor lass felt her heart turn over. 'I wass thinking,' she said, 'where there iss a wull there iss a way. Old Chacob hass not told you efferything.'

'What hass he not been telling me?' asked Erchie sharply. He saw the friendly light in the girl's eye, and took a quick note of her points, as if she were a ship, and his heart turned over.

'He did not tell you that he cannot abide the worms eating his corp, so he had a lead coffin made for himself at Inverness and delivered here a month ago.'

'Cot bless my soul! A lead coffin! Och well, he has a

good right to it if he wants it. But what has that got to do with his wull—Catriona?' He lingered over the name, liking the sound of it.

'There iss no one else at Screavie knows of the coffin except me. I want you to make me a promise. It iss most important. You must not mention the lead coffin to anyone before Chacob's funeral—better not even to Tougal. Will you make that promise?'

'Indeed yess, since you think it's important.'

'Then I advise you to become Chacob's heir. If you cannot keep it, I advise you not to.'

'Well, now, here iss a mystery! You cannot be leaving me in the air like this, Catriona.'

'Ask me no more chust now, Erchie. My own mind iss not clear. I will haff to think.'

'I will be seeing you again, sometime, lass. You will be telling me when the time is right.' Erchie could draw nothing more out of Catriona that night. He rowed back over the loch to rejoin his birthday party. When they asked him what old Jacob had been wanting, he replied, 'Chacob thinks he iss dying and wass saying goodbye.' But after the men were gone he was telling all to Dougal. 'Yon Catriona iss a bonnie lass. I am liking her fine. She advises me to accept the condeetions, but what sort of a life would that be? Me the laughing-stock of the village, up there at the kirkyard each morning. Neffer could I go away even for a day, except for that one month a year. And what if I wass wanting to marry a lass? Fair tormented I would be, aal for a scantling of money—and what use iss that if I am pinned down like a butterfly in a gless case?'

'Aye,' said Dougal, 'a sore dilemma it iss, but count the blessings too. You could fit out a proper fushing boat with enchines and aal—think of an eighty-eight horse-power Kelvin diesel—instead of your two rowing boats and one with a rotting bottom. It iss a fleet you could buy, if you wished.'

'Och, it iss not big business I want. One fushing smack would do me, and the nets, and a new van, and maybe a car, and a good chetty, aye, and a boat-house, and crew, and I've aye had a mind for a house with bow windows. In winter I could do with an inside closet—and electric power, and—'

'You'd better say yess to old Chacob,' concluded Dougal. 'If you want a lass too, maybe you could be haffing her but not marry, the same as you haff aalways done before.'

This was a bold new notion to Erchie. He gave it thought, then added. 'I haff been sorry you were not knowing your own mother, Tougal.'

'Aye,' said Dougal, 'but that iss chust the way of it. . . . I would neffer marry myself.'

'Would you not, now? Indeed aye, yess, indeed,' was all Erchie could say. For he was thinking.

Next day he was over the loch to tell Jacob he would be his heir, and that night before dark he had a long walk with Catriona by the shore. Every night for a week after that he was meeting her for ten minutes, for the old man could not be left. The more the two met, the deeper grew their mutual admiration. He was taken with her quick mind and modesty, she with his slow mind and sureness. Och, the pair were made for each other. In no time at all they were head over heels in love.

One Monday morning, two weeks later, news came to Screavie that old Jacob had died in the night. On Tuesday the undertaker's men came from Inverness to coffin the body. That same day Erchie had a letter from Jacob's lawyers to say that after the funeral on Friday the will would be read at the manse: he must be there to hear it at 4 p.m., on peril of losing great benefits if he failed.

On Thursday, Erchie had a visit from the Reverend

73

Dr Micheal MacLeod. 'Erchie,' said he, 'Catriona of Glen Dearg has chust been to see me. She tells me that Mr Frewin made a last request on his death-bed. Since his own living had been made off the sea and ships, he wanted his dead body to travel by sea to the grave. He asked that you should be ferryman, to bring his body across Loch Screavie to the north shore, where the mourners would be meeting it for the last lift to the kirkyard. It iss a noble and simple wish—if a wee thing unusual like the dead man himself. Sure I am that you will be willing to grant it. Will you do it?'

Erchie agreed at once and times were fixed.

At one o'clock on Friday, Erchie and Dougal had the boat at the jetty by Screavie House. Catriona had asked Jamie Urquhart, the Earl's head keeper, for help with the lead coffin. Two ghillies, and two shepherds, and two sweating undertaker's men, carried it down to the beach.

'What iss thiss?' cried Erchie. 'A lead coffin! Lead! By chove, what a terrible weight it must be! If I had been told I would haff brought my bigger boat.'

'Och, Dougal will help at the oaring,' said Jamie. 'But look you! there iss a bit wind out on the water.'

The men had a hard job lowering the coffin aboard. It could not go longways, because that left no vacant thwart for the oarsmen, and if moved aft it sank the stern too low. It had to be laid across the gunwales, projecting over each side.

'I will haff to row her chust by myself,' declared Erchie. 'She iss low enough in the water as she iss, without another man aboard.'

'That boat iss not safe,' warned Jamie.

'Och,' said Catriona, 'it is a keeper you are, not a sailor. Erchie will manage fine.'

'Chust a capful of wind,' said Dougal, averting his eyes.

'I will do my best,' promised Erchie. 'Dougal, go you

round quick to the north shore, and row out my other boat, chust in case.'

They waited while he pushed off from the jetty. All was well, for he was under the lee of the hills, but farther out it was rougher. Then they all scrambled aboard the estate's two Land Rovers and drove fast round the loch to the cottage. Dougal slipped the moorings of the bigger boat and Niall Cameron the policeman took an oar with him.

By this time Erchie was half way across. 'His boat looks terrible low in the water,' said Niall. 'I hope she will not be sinking.'

'Aye,' replied Dougal, 'a lead coffin will be putting the creatt strain on her timbers, which are not aal that sound. It iss shameful that no one warned Erchie in good time.'

Dougal kept looking over his shoulder to watch. 'He has stopped rowing,' he reported. 'He iss bending down, trying to do something at the bottom of the boat. . . . Row, Niall man, row! His boat is down to the gunwales!'

They heard a cry. When they looked, Erchie was standing up pulling off his thigh-boots. Next moment the coffin slipped over the side and the boat capsized.

They reached him inside a couple of minutes and none too soon. He was holding to the upturned boat, but the cold was fearsome. When they pulled him aboard he gasped (never a thought for himself), 'The coffin, the coffin! It iss away to Tavy Chones! What will the poor meenister do for a funeral?'

'Stop you!' said Niall. 'The Refferent MacLeod will be thinking what I am thinking. There iss aalways the whusky.'

'Niall Cameron!' rebuked Erchie, 'it iss ill to be choking before the service iss spoken.'

'Och, man,' said Niall, 'since when wass whusky not a serious subchect?' He fetched a flask from his hip pocket and passed it over. 'Take a wee droppie on your tongue before you catch your death.'

Erchie took a pull that made Niall wince, then drew breath and said, 'I am chust thinking, maybe it iss a good thing the coffin iss lead or no one would want my fush next week.'

He made fast the upturned boat with a rope to its transom-ring, at the same time, unseen by Niall, pushing the cork he had in his hand back into the plug-hole in the bottom. 'Row hard, man!' he commanded, 'before the fire in me dies.'

As they towed the boat ashore all Screavie was collecting on the beach. The Reverend Dr MacLeod was the first to greet them when they grounded.

'The Lord be praised, Mr MacFarlane, at least you are safe! We are spared a double funeral. The coffin—' he whispered as Dougal stumbled ashore (the whisky was taking effect)—'it has gone to the bottom?'

'Aye, Dr MacLeod. Fifty fathoms down.'

'In heaven's name!' commanded the Earl of Ewe, 'how could this come to happen?'

'A lead coffin, my lord. And me neffer guessing took over the smaller of my two boats. She wass overloaded, an' taking water over the bows at mid-stream. Then she sprang a leak,

". . . and afore you knowed,

She filled by the head and down she goed."'

'It was like Jacob to end this way,' said the Earl to the minister. 'Always he went too deep to be reached by his kin. Now he's three hundred feet under. I propose we go out to mid-loch and hold the funeral service there. I'll take out my motor-cruiser. You fetch yours, Drumgast. Between us we can lift thirty people. Quite enough.'

No other course was open. Old Jacob must rest forever

where he was. Erchie went off to change into dry clothes—
no one had noticed that he was not wearing his Sunday suit
—and to warm his bones with a second dram. Meanwhile
the funeral went ahead, with the chief mourners out on the
water and the rest of Screavie lining the beach. Aye, what
a day for the gossip it was! Nothing like this had happened
since the ghost of Sandy MacTavish had come back from
Australia.

At four sharp Erchie was up at the manse. Beside the
lawyer from Inverness, there were the Earl and Countess of
Ewe, the Reverend Dr MacLeod, and Erchie. The Earl
looked surprised to see Erchie, and when the will was read
his face was a study. Erchie had the grace to look dumbfounded.

'This should be one of the best jokes of my life,' confessed the Earl, 'were it not that I can't raise a laugh. . . . Do
you accept your very awkward position, Mr MacFarlane?'

Erchie kept them on tenterhooks for a full quarter-
minute. Then, 'I do, my lord,' said he. 'Except that my
daily prayer at the kirkyard has been taken from me.'

'You will have to go out into the middle of the loch and
pray there.'

'The wull says no such thing,' said Erchie firmly. 'It says
"by my grave in the Screavie kirkyard." Since he iss not
there I cannot go. Otherwise the wull stands.'

'Mr MacFarlane is right,' agreed the lawyer. 'The detail
about the kirkyard was clearly most important in the
Honourable Jacob Frewin's mind, but a stroke of Providence
has struck it out. We must accept what remains of the will.'

'I argue,' said the minister, 'that Mr Frewin's wish would
haff been that failing the kirkyard the daily prayer be said
out on the loch.'

'Chust that!' exclaimed Erchie. 'It iss mere speculation.
Here are the terms of the wull, which iss aal we know of

Mr Frewin's mind. Take it as it iss, and not read into it more than it says. We must fulfil what iss left to fulfil and leave what cannot be. Aye, we could argue till we were black in the face, go to the courts and be paying lawyers for the rest of our days, aal to their benefit and none to ours. Chentlemen, if you can agree with me you will be finding me more chenerous to the kirk than Dr MacLeod dreams.'

The minister perked up at that, the Earl looked glum. There was more argument, but the lawyer ruled that no one was entitled to re-write the will to offset an act of God, which was what the loss of coffin and contents amounted to, and which they must accept. This was the point that finally silenced the minister. It did cross the Earl's mind that Erchie had sunk the coffin deliberately, then he remembered that Erchie had not known the terms of the will, as well the Earl had seen by his face—just an unsophisticated fisherman.

So Erchie won the day. Great was the pride he had ever after in Catriona. A smart lass yon! They came to an understanding. Erchie moved across the loch to Screavie House and Catriona stayed on as his housekeeper. Aye, and when they lay in bed or looked out across the water from the windows (and they were bow windows), many were the prayers they said for the rest of old Jacob's bones.

WILD CAT

8

EARLY one morning in May, young Dougal MacFarlane made fast his ferry alongside two fishing boats from Ullapool, which had put in to the Cairnban jetty at sunrise. The crews were wanting bread, and to mend and clean nets. So Dougal and they were sitting on the jetty, chaffing each other and enjoying the sun, for there was not a cloud in the sky. The water shone bright with colour from the hillsides —old and new greens of pine and larch, old and new bracken, and down at the sea's edge a blaze of yellow broom and gorse. A peacock's tail has less colour than Loch Screavie in May.

'Och, Dougal,' says one of the men, 'this iss not the place for a lad like you. It iss at Ullapool you should be, earning a good wage at the fushing.'

'Leave the poor lad alone,' says another. 'Maybe he iss chust born lazy. If a man likes doing nothing, why should he not, tell me that? It iss the chief occupation at Screavie, save for one other. Aye, and who can blame them? Not me, I can tell you. There iss more bonnie lasses at Screavie than anywhere else on the west coast.'

'You haff hit the nail there,' says a third. 'Wass it chust the laziness in young Tougal, he might be sitting there on the chetty as now but not at eight in the morning. No, no, it iss a lass that keep him at Screavie. . . . Look you at the flush on his face, even to his ears! Aye, aye, it is a lucky lass she iss, and him getting aal he iss wanting. He chust cannot tear himself away.'

'Ach, it iss not that at aal,' says the first. 'Many a time we haff looked in at Screavie ceilidhs, yet how much headway haff we made with the lasses? Bonnie enough they are, but smert, smert.'

'They would haff to be that,' says the second, 'with Tougal on their laps.'

'Chust what I meant,' says the first. 'Remember yon wild cat from Glen Dorcha?—the bonniest red-head in Ross, but aal spit and scratch. Effery man that looked near her wass sent off sudden with a flea in his ear! Poor Tougal iss here not because he gets aal he iss wanting, but because he does not. And look you, still he stays on, a thrawn lad.'

The incessant teasing suddenly became more than Dougal could stand. He jumped up and stalked shoreward, his hands thrust deep in his trouser pockets, his eyes downcast and sullen. A year ago he had opened this ferry service from Cairnban at the mouth of Loch Screavie to Liabaig on its south shore, using an old thirty-foot motor-boat given by Erchie, his father. He plied a good trade in summer between the inns on either side. 'The tourist iss neffer content with where he iss now, but aye must be going to where he iss not,' explained Dougal, shaking his head at southern daftness. In the off-season he made just three crossings a day, morning, noon, and evening. Always he had passengers—there was no motor-road along the south shore to link Screavie with Liabaig.

A car drove up as Dougal reached the end of the jetty. The Reverend Dr MacLeod stepped out of one door, and Angus of the Glens from the other. 'Ferryman,' cried Angus, 'you haff three customers this morning.'

'Good day to you, Dougal,' said the Reverend MacLeod. 'I am stopping overnight at Liabaig and not back till the morn. Angus here iss away down the coast to Kyle.'

'Aye,' said Dougal shortly, still feeling sore. 'It will be a fine day for you both. Who iss my third passencher?'

'Morag of Glen Dorcha,' said MacLeod. 'She's coming up on her bike.'

The three of them walked up to the jetty to exchange a word with the Ullapool men, then clambered across the fishing boats to the ferry. 'Dougal,' said Dr MacLeod, 'Morag iss to collect a bale of Harris wool sent up from Kyle for her weaving. Now, to save her the chourney, would you not collect it yourself? It iss to lie overnight in the shed here by the chetty. In the morn I'll bring it down to Screavie on the roof of my car.'

'I will if she'll let me,' answered Dougal doubtfully.

Angus laughed. 'It iss not Morag will let any man help her, and well you know it, Dougal. I would offer myself, but she'd bite my nose off.'

'Perhaps Dougal iss different,' ventured Dr MacLeod, remembering well that Angus had once gone three years with Morag.

Angus shook his head. 'She and Dougal haff been friends since they were at school, yet the guard she keeps would defeat a Don Chuan. Many's the man would like to be courting that lass. You ask Dougal.'

'I would not be knowing,' snapped Dougal.

Oho! thought MacLeod, so that iss how it iss. He turned to Angus. 'What troubles her? I know her mother is bad with arthritis, but Morag has character. She weaves the tweed and tries hard to make a living of a kind. A man could be a help to them both. Why does she not marry?'

Angus shrugged. 'A fine voice she has too, but would not sing at a ceilidh this winter nor dance at the village hall

—nor talk at aal to a man save he wass old enough to be nigh dead.'

'Chust that! Angus, she speaks to me.'

'I meant dead to this world,' explained Angus quickly.

Dougal's face lit of a sudden as they heard an Ullapool man exclaim, 'Cot bless my soul! The wild cat of Screavie!'

She had left her bike by the road and was walking up the jetty—Morag of Glen Dorcha—she of the hair red as the Cuillin at sunset, and her skin like the wild bees' honey, and the eyes of her green as Loch Scavaig.

'Good morning, Morag,' shouted one of the fishermen. 'It iss a fine day this.'

She gave a defiant toss to her head and walked on, not giving the men a look. It was what they expected and all were exchanging smiles. As she scrambled across their boats to the ferry, one of them gave her a muted wolf whistle. Her eye was scornful.

'Good morning, Morag,' said the minister. 'Dougal here is going to lift your wool from the shed at Liabaig. That will save you the chourney over the loch.'

'Thank you, I will manache myself.'

'Come, Morag. There iss no need to be paying five shillings for the crossing if you let Dougal pick up the wool.'

'I am also to veesit my sister at Liabaig,' declared Morag. 'I will not be coming back till this evening.'

'Och,' said Dougal, 'I will not be asking a fare if you are chust veesiting your sister.'

'I want no favours, thank you. Here iss your fare.' Morag held out the money, but Dougal made no move. She put down the money beside him. He picked up his sweater and spread it on the stern seat near the tiller. 'You sit here, Morag,' said he.

'I like to sit on bare wood,' replied Morag, and sat down beside Dr MacLeod.

Dougal's face darkened. He started up his engine, cast off, and took the tiller. The ferry-boat chugged out from the jetty. The Ullapool men gave them a wave and one a good-humoured cat-call.

'Look—that wass a salmon chumped!' cried MacLeod.

'It was a fush,' said Dougal.

Angus moved aft beside him.

'Morag,' said MacLeod, 'how iss your mother keeping?'

'She hass difficulty moving about, but things are getting better—I haff sales for my tweed.'

'Has she long to wait for the old age pension?'

'She hass long. She would fare ill if effer I left her.'

The Reverend MacLeod sat up. 'Iss that why you take such a defiant way with the young men?'

'It iss not.'

The minister examined Dougal sitting by the tiller. The boy had a fine head on him, jet black hair with a brown skin, a quick smile when he was not cast down as now. 'He iss a fine lad, that, Morag. Full of speerit. You spoke sherp, sherp, when he tried to please you.'

'He is like aal the rest. I want help from none of them.'

'Now that iss not a chust thing to say. It iss a bold eye he hass, and times he may be mischievous with the girls— but young men are like that: it iss not really a fault, it iss natural.'

'I want nothing from any of them.'

'Morag, Morag, why think ill of them? The Ullapool men are calling you the wild cat of Screavie—and you with the looks that could turn their herts.'

Morag spoke sharply. 'I will be haffing no man about me. I haff seen what they're like.'

The minister sighed. 'Men and women are made to help each other.'

'Help, did you say! There iss Angus MacGregor, sitting

83

at the stern of this boat. He used to be crossing the bealach on Sundays to see me in Glen Dorcha. Three years we went together, till we came to an understanding. Suddenly he came no more. The only word I had wass a letter, to say I wass his half-sister. Then I learned he wass not my half-brother, because old Murdo MacGregor, who was indeed my father, wass not his father after all. The man I had thought wass my father, and who marrit my mother, emigrated to Canada. He wass to send for us aal later, but eighteen years haff passed with not one line from him. My sister Sheila has had to stay with my aunt at Liabaig.'

Some of this was news even to the Reverend MacLeod. 'Morag, that iss a terrible story.'

'I am wanting no men about me.'

After a short pause Dr MacLeod asked, 'Did you know Dougal has suffered likewise? His mother ran off before Erchie could marry her.' A flicker of interest came to her eye, and he added, 'Dougal still likes women.'

While the minister pled in vain, Angus was having a word with Dougal at the stern. 'Morag never used to be like this. It has come on in the last year or two.'

'The hert of her has turned to stone.'

'Och, a soft hert she has, Dougal—but she's built a stone-dyke round it. Yet there wass neffer a dyke and no way over it. Here iss a hint I can give you: don't try to persuade her she needs you; make her feel it iss you needs her. Aye, that iss a part of the answer. She needs to be needed. That's one of her main traits—she'd haff been off to the nursing long ago if her mother had been fit.'

' "Let pain and anguish wring the brow?" ' suggested Dougal.

Angus looked doubtful. 'It would haff to be something sudden, as unlooked for as snow in Chuly, to make an anchel of Morag.'

When they reached Liabaig the tide was high and they came in at the jetty (which dries on the ebb). Dougal jumped ashore and made fast. He held out an arm to Morag. She ignored him as usual. He had been noting the state of the tide and an idea was shaping in his head. 'You are certain to be coming this evening, Morag?'

'On the five o'clock ferry.'

'I am sorry—today it hass to be four o'clock.'

'Oh, well, I will be here at four.' She moved off with never a look.

The minister was met by parishioners, and Angus hurried off to catch the bus south. A steep hill led up to the road, where Liabaig Inn stood with the village spreading to either side. Beyond lay a swell of heathery moorland, rising to mountains. Dougal stood by the jetty, as if admiring the view, but in truth admiring Morag's easy swing from the hip as she climbed the track to the roadside, where she turned to look back on the loch. Their eyes met. She turned hastily away, hoping he had not thought—. But Dougal was thinking.

When she had disappeared, he walked into the post office and wrote out a notice: *Ferry service to Cairnban cancelled for today, 25th May, after 3 p.m.* He had this stuck on the window, and then went straight to the bus-shed. He picked up Morag's wool—an eighty-pound bale—and carried it down to the boat, where there were half a dozen passengers waiting.

All day long the sun was flooding out of the sky, and the land greedy for warmth yielded every scent and colour: on all sides there was this profusion of giving and yielding up. It was the perfect day for making love, and Dougal in despair at the dour heart of one woman. Or maybe not yet in despair. He spent lunchtime in his caravan reading his *Ship Captain's Medical Guide.*

85

At a quarter to four, he was waiting again by the Liabaig jetty, this time wearing a clean white shirt with his sleeves rolled up. Above him, on the back veranda of the inn, which overlooked the loch and a garden, Euan MacKay the inn-keeper was sunning himself. He called Dougal in, as if just for a word on the fine weather, but after a few minutes he said, 'A wee bit rumour comes to my ear that maybe old Chacob Frewin has left your father a pickle of money. Not that I am asking, you know, for I would not do that, but chust wondering if there would be any truth in it.'

'If Wullie the Post says it, it must be true,' acknowledged Dougal, grinning. 'Aye, there iss a grain of truth in it this time.'

'Erchie has taken Screavie House—will that not take a lot to keep up?'

'Och, he can afford that and more.'

'By chove, this will be good news for you, Dougal! You will surely not keep on at the ferry, and be living in that caravan at Cairnban?'

For the first time Dougal's flinty eye sparked. 'It iss boats I want to build,' he said eagerly. 'Boats are the most perfect things man makes. Not power-boats, mark you, but sailing boats. In Chuly I am off to the Clyde to a yacht-yard. In September I begin full training.'

'Creatt news, Tougal, creatt news!' Euan jumped up and called through the door to a lass, 'Bring my Screavie whusky and the crystal glesses, quick now!' To Dougal, 'This iss on the house.'

'Stop you!' exclaimed Dougal. 'Here iss Morag coming down to the ferry. Would you be minding if she choined us?'

At once Euan gave a shout, 'Morag! Come and take a dram with Tougal and me. We haff a toast to give you.'

Morag stopped and shook her head. She advanced reluctantly to the garden wall and said, 'Thank you, Mr

86

MacKay, I will go to the ferry and wait.' In the face of all his protestations she turned and walked off. Euan shrugged his shoulders. Dougal took a big whisky instead of a small. Euan gave him a toast: 'Boats, and the men who build them!'

'In time I'll build my own,' added Dougal, 'not chust work for other men.'

'*Slainté!*'

Dougal walked down to the ferry. The tide was nearly full out, as he had planned, and the butt-end of the jetty high and dry. He had therefore moored the boat at a buoy and had come ashore in a dinghy, which now lay on the beach, with Morag standing beside it.

'Where iss my wool?' she demanded.

'I took it on my last crossing. It wass too heavy for a woman, Morag.'

'I could haff lifted it.'

He said nothing, but dragged the dinghy over the shingle into the water. The beach had little shelving and the boat's stern now lay three or four paces out in the water.

'Iss there no other passencher?' asked Morag in dismay.

'It seems you're the only one. I will carry you out.'

'You will not lay a hand on me, Dougal MacFarlane. I will take my bare feet.'

'Nonsense! I haff carried the meenister before this, and Chanet Dunbar, forbye.'

'But not me.'

'You are to be carried,' said Dougal. Before she knew he had stooped and lifted her up by legs and back. 'Do not kick, wuman!'

'Put me down!'

He held her the tighter and quickly carried her to the boat. He pushed off and jumped in himself. She said nothing more, but sat tense and resentful. The only sound was the creak of oars in rowlocks, and the dip of blades, and seagulls crying. When they came alongside the ferry-boat he did not offer a hand, nor in truth did she need one. But frustration deepened in him, just watching her do without.

While the boat went *chug-chugging* out from Liabaig, dinghy in tow, the pair sat silent and moody. As soon as they neared the middle of the loch, Dougal opened a locker and brought out a thermos flask and a box. 'Morag,' said he, 'will you please share a cup of tea? I haff sugar and milk and some shortbread.'

She let fall an indifferent glance on his offering, then continued to gaze over his head at the blue hills, and stayed silent.

'Morag, the day iss beautiful, the ferry's early. Haff one cup with me, and a bite to eat. It will freshen you for the hill track to Glen Dorcha.'

'Thank you, I am not hungry.'

'Well, chust haff the tea. I am not wanting to drink it alone.'

'I haff not a thirst on me.'

'Morag—I brought it for you. Please haff something. The tea iss not long made.'

'I said no.'

'Morag, there iss a new tin of shortbread here, unopened. Would you take it for your mother? I would like her to haff it.' Dougal rose, and offered the tin with a smile. 'Please—take it for your mother.'

'I can take no presents, thank you.'

Dougal returned to the tiller, crestfallen. He was silent for a minute. Then he said, 'I would like you to be my friend, as you used to be.'

'Why should I? You or any man.'

'I am not any man. I haff known you aal my life.'

'Well, I do not want you for a friend.'

88

It was the first time she had outspokenly rejected him. Making no allowances, Dougal flared up, hot-eyed. 'Nor do I want you for a friend: I want you for love! Are you blind, wuman?'

Beside himself, he switched off the engine and went to her side. 'You treat me like a boy, who iss not to speak till spoken to. Morag, it iss a man I am, and you a wuman. I will not haff you play with me.' He seized her by the shoulders and planted an angry kiss on her cheek. He stepped back then, to let her strike him as anticipated, but was startled by the mad look in her eye. Quick as thought, she snatched up the boat-hook and slammed him over the head. He half fell across the centre thwart, stepped up on it as if to jump aft, when she struck him again on the side. He was alert and let himself topple across the gunwale. His shoulder struck it with a thud and he rolled overboard.

'Dougal!' cried Morag in panic.

He was splashing in the water, holding with one hand to the edge of the dinghy. Hurt as he might be, he never lost his self-possession. Morag was looking anxiously over the side. 'Can you get back?' she asked.

'My shoulder,' he gasped. 'Broken! I cannot pull out. If I let go, my sea-boots will drown me.' His face twisted.

'What will I do?' she beseeched.

'Pull in the dinghy to midships.'

She took the painter and towed the dinghy into position.

'Be quick!' gasped Dougal. 'Step into the dinghy and help me over its stern.'

She stepped down and took a grip of his shirt collar.

'Keep to centre,' he cautioned, 'or you will be capsizing the boat. When I count three, pull hard and sudden.'

He counted, and heaved up on his right arm as she pulled. Next moment his shirt tore off across his back, but his body was sprawled half over the transom. He lay for a moment, eyes closed. She examined him carefully, supporting his head and shoulders on her knees. 'Dougal!' she cried. . . . 'Oh dear, haff you fainted away?' She placed her hands on either side of his bare chest to pull him farther inboard.

Dougal stirred. 'It iss chust dizzy I am. It iss my shoulder. In a moment I will be aal right.'

Morag pulled the dinghy alongside the motor-boat and helped Dougal aboard.

'Your arm,' she asked, 'iss it really broken?'

He felt it over. 'The shoulder iss dislocated. I haff to support the arm aal the time.'

'How do you know it iss dislocated?'

'The elbow sticks out. I can feel the bone at my arm-pit.'

Morag felt in despair. 'What can we *do*?'

'It iss aal right, Morag. I know what to do, if you help me.' He drew a knife from his belt and cut away the remains of his shirt. 'I must lie flat,' he said, 'and get you to pull my arm.'

He lay flat on the boards of the boat. 'Now take off your left shoe, put your heel into my arm-pit, grasp my hand and elbow, and pull.'

She did as he said, sitting beside him. 'Do I pull hard?' she asked fearfully.

'Pull steady—go on!'

His shoulder, which had been held high, suddenly jumped back to normal. 'You haff done it, Morag!' he cried joyfully. No doctor could haff done it better! Thank you. I would haff been quite helpless without you, and drowned in the sea, forbye.'

'Iss there much pain?' asked Morag quickly, feeling an unwelcome warmth on her cheek.

'Aye, there iss an ache,' he grimaced. 'It will not be too bad if I can let it lie still for a day or two. Could you help me again, Morag, by making a sling from my shirt?'

While she was busy folding the cloth, he added, 'Morag —it is sorry I am I took hold of you. I chust could not help that kiss. I wass feeling so baffled I chust lost my head. Unless I kissed you then I felt I neffer would again.... But that iss the end of it, Morag. You will be right neffer to look at me—but please forgive me, at least in your hert.'

'Here iss the shirt.' Morag's tone was distant. 'Fold your arm across the chest. . . . Now turn round and I will be tying the knot. . . . There!'

She went to the thermos flask and poured out two cups of tea, and gave him one. They drank and ate. Dougal dared not believe his good fortune: for a few minutes his hopes ran high. She had spoken kindly, been gentle, taken his food and drink. He had to re-start the engine. From that moment till she stepped ashore at the Cairnban jetty she said little else. When he tried to talk she made a sign to him to be quiet, and just stared out over the sea, her face pale, her eyes showing a mind far distant from any boat at the mouth of Loch Screavie.

They moored the ferry off Cairnban. When he set her ashore, she turned on the jetty and said, 'Be careful with that arm,' and went off, not using his name or looking him once in the eye. He stared after her, and this time his anguish was real. He watched her walk quickly to the road-side, pick up her bike, mount, and ride off without a backward glance.

Five minutes later he was back in his caravan. Sun and blue sky, sea and hills, even the cuckoos calling from the birchwoods, all were lost to him, things of no joy. He looked around him in disgust. 'Home sweet home,' thought he bitterly. 'Home!' He banged the table with a clenched fist. 'I've never had one! This iss chust a grave! My hert dead as hers. I haff no wish to live or build boats, or to learn anything. What would be the use? Aal iss empty, empty, *empty*!'

Ignoring his wet clothes, he sat for twenty minutes, his mind blank as the walls of his caravan, his hert as heavy as Jacob's lead coffin. He heard a step outside, and a knock at his door. In a small, flat voice he said, 'Who iss there?' adding with an ill-grace, 'Come in.'

It was Morag. So quick are a man's reactions at nineteen that Dougal leapt to his feet, on the instant fully alive.

'I haff been to the Cairnban store,' announced Morag, 'and bought you cloth for a sling and codeine for the pain. Forbye, I had better help you on with a clean shirt.'

Donald looked guilty. 'That wass the clean one, that wass. . . . Och, but there iss one not too bad.' He opened a locker and picked one out.

Morag looked pleasantly surprised. 'You keep the place tidy—efferything stowed neatly, like a ship. . . . And these books on the shelf—' she looked close—'Navigation— Boat-building—Sailing. You read these?'

'I know them by hert,' said Dougal proudly.

She helped him on with his shirt and fixed the sling. Her eyes lifted to the pin-ups on the wall.

'Och,' said Dougal, 'it iss aalways some company, when there's no one else.'

'Dougal!' said Morag sharply, 'change your trousers before you catch your death of cold. It iss not good for you, standing there. Now, I think that is aal I can do. I will go—' and she turned away to the door.

'Thank you Morag.' His heart sank. 'Will I neffer see you again?'

'You cannot be running the ferry with one arm—so I will be here effery morning till your arm iss better, chust to help. I will not haff you starving. You are needing me now.'

'Morag—'

'I will come back in five meenutes,' she interrupted, 'if you want me to come—?'

'I do want!'

'Oh, Dougal! I haff tried not to love you, because I felt so much in danger of it. But when the sea nearly took you I saw it wass no use. I will be coming back chust to let you kiss me properly.'

Dougal did not wait to change his trousers. His arm was round her, then his other arm too, and Morag never even noticed.

THE WATER OF LIFE

9

THE illicit still at Screavie first arose out of dire necessity, and was not run as now from anger at excessive taxation. The lads had come home at the end of the war. Imagine their dismay when nowhere could be found a drop of *uisque beatha*! Nor at first could they see a promise of it. Where could a still be sited, unless the laird, active on the hills, clapped telescope to blind eye? Where could the money be raised to buy the gear? Who at Screavie knew the art of distilling, or even how to assemble a still?—not one. The men were in despair. But aye Providence will send the agents to fulfil her will.

In its early days, the still came to be sited in a cave in Coire Garbh, under the Bealach Dubh. Many a ceilidh the men had there, and many a hundred bottles sailed off to Gairloch and Ullapool aboard Erchie MacFarlane's fishing boat. Not even Glenlivet surpassed the Screavie spirit when matured. It cannot be said where the present site may be, but then as now all ceilidhs opened with a toast to the first agents of Providence, the Fairy King and the Real MacKay. 'You might be wondering who these chentlemen are?' Wullie the Post will say if you ask him. 'Oich! oich! It iss the creatt mystery that iss in it. But it chust so happens that you haff asked the right person, becoss I haff met them both myself.'

It was the year of the Great Thirst. Donald MacPherson,

who had been demobilized a year before, was now head keeper to Sir John Drumgast. The two of them met this May morning on the lawn before the big house, and were standing together under a silver spruce. 'I never thocht I'd live to see the day,' lamented Johnnie, 'when there'd no' be a drap o' the cratur in all of Ross! Man wis no' meant to live withoot whusky. The Guid Book itself says it: "Go thy ways, eat thy breid wi' joy, and drink thy wine wi' a merry hert." ' He sighed—and forgetting that he was a laird and a J.P.—'A wonder it is the lads dinna put their heids together. There's nae lack o' cruminal talent in Screavie.'

Donald gave him a right sharp look, to see if the laird was joking. But Johnnie Drumgast was never the man to joke about whisky. Donald decided to make a long cast, and in all the length and breadth of Ross there was no man could cast a fly like him. 'Och, they're law-abiding lads at Loch Screavie,' said he, knowing well that up in Coire Garbh, on the laird's own land, a cave that might house a still was being prospected. 'It iss the creatt respect they aal haff for an exciseman. Forbye, the herts of them are set on the Real MacKay, and that would need money. They would haff nothing less than a pot still, and no use for aught save barley malt, aye, and that sprouted and cured only over peat fires—and a cask or two, so that whateffer might not be consumed now would mature in the fullness of time. Idealists they are, seeking a true bouquet and a full ethereal flavour.'

Sir John changed colour as the image rose before his eyes, and the bouquet to his nose. '*Uisque b'a*,' he crooned, his voice trembling. 'It is the water of life. Man, man,' he groaned, 'you are sore tormenting me.'

'It iss me that iss thinking,' said Donald softly, not to Sir John, but as if to the silver spruce overhead, 'thinking of a line from the Good Book to match your own: "Wine maketh merry; but money answereth aal things." '

Sir John lifted up his head like a stag scenting, then looked far away to the rims of the hills, just as if he had not heard, and there was a long pause. . . . 'How much?' he whispered, not to Donald, but as if communicating with the hills themselves. 'I am wondering how much would answer for a Screavie whusky?'

'It iss not me would be knowing a thing like that, Sir Chohn. Indeed, no. . . . Two hundred pounds, I haff heard tell, would buy aal the gear needed.'

Johnnie was staring up into the branches. 'Dae ye believe in the fairies?' he asked absent-like, yet not as if changing the subject.

'I believe in the fairies,' declared Donald firmly.

'Go you then to the bottom o' the gairden. Say it aloud three times. Then say to yourself in silence: "I wish a wish that Sir John Drumgast be sent a bottle of *uisque b'a* once a week frae the fairy still, so long as a still is there." Then come back in ten minutes to this very spot. I'll wager you find a crock of gold under the silver spruce.'

Donald went off and did as he was told. When he came back, Sir John had vanished, but there under the spruce lay a heap of forty five-pound notes with a stone on top. That is why, to this very day, a toast to the Fairy King is drunk at the Screavie still.

The toast to the Real MacKay demands some subtlety of understanding. The territory of Clan MacAoidh is Sutherland. It was they invented whisky when they came with the Scots from Dalriada in the sixth century, but the toast is not to the chief of that clan, no, indeed. Nor to his forebears. It is to a spirit, aye, and it can possess and inspire a man as well as a whisky, and come and go as it wills like a Muse.

When the war ended, the Navy had ships lying off Loch Ewe. While the men waited for demobilisation the Navy tried to find local jobs for sailors wanting training in the work they might go to when freed. By arrangement with the Reverend Alasdair MacColl of Ullapool, Donald MacPherson was brought up from Screavie to interview the men. His talent in acting the apoplectic dragon had made him the perfect regimental sergeant-major in a famous Highland regiment. That fierce eye of his, and the hook-nose like an eagle's, meant there would be no nonsense from the men off the ships. He would see to that—and put fear of sudden death into sailors not too willing to work as he did into ghillies. Forbye, no one knew better than he where jobs could be found in Wester Ross.

They gave him an office near the quay and three petty officers to help. On that first day, thirty sailors were lined up at the door, and Donald had them in one by one to hear what their former work had been.

The first man to stump in was a thin-faced, sandy-haired lad with a squint.

'What would be the name of you?' asked Donald.

'MacKay, sir. Jock MacKay.'

Donald wrote it down. 'Now, be telling me what wass your chob.'

'Socktuckersir.'

'A what—?'

'Socktuckersir.'

Donald gave him a sharp look. 'Spell it,' says he.

'S-o-c-k-t-u-c-k-e-r, sir.'

'A sock tucker! Iss that what you were saying?'

'Yessir.'

'Now,' demanded Donald, 'will you be telling me what in the name of Satan iss a sock tucker?'

'Yessir. I used to work in a woollen factory making socks by machine. My job was to put tucks in the heel.'

'Chust that! Chust that!' Donald took his particulars

97

and sent him away, he dragging his heels as much as he dared, now that the war was over.

'Next man!' cried a petty officer.

The second man was a thick-set tar, as small and black as a Pict, and dour in the face.

'Your name?' asked Donald.

'MacKay, sir. Aeneas MacKay.'

Donald wrote it down. 'MacKay. Will you be any relation to the MacKay that wass in ahead of you?'

'Nosir. No relation sir.'

'What iss your chob?'

'Cokesackersir.'

'A what—?'

'Cokesackersir.'

Donald drew down shaggy brows and gave the man a fierce look. 'Spell it.'

'C-o-k-e-s-a-c-k-e-r, sir.'

'A coke sacker—iss that what you are telling me?'

'Yessir.'

'A coke sacker,' muttered Donald heavily. 'What in the name of aal the deffils of hell iss a coke sacker? Will you be telling me that?'

'Well, sir, I worked in a gas works. When the coal is heated it becomes coke. My job was to shovel the coke into sacks.'

'Would you be telling me that, now? So, it iss a coke sacker you are!' Donald took down all his particulars and sent him away.

'Next man!' cried the petty officer.

The third rating slouched in. He was round as a tub with cheeks shining like apples and eyes bright as buttons.

'Straighten that back!' barked Donald. 'Pull in that belly! . . . What name, man?'

'MacKay, sir.'

Donald's nostrils distended. 'Cot bless my soul! Not another MacKay! Iss it all the MacKays of Sutherland that are here?'

'My name's MacKay, sir. Daniel MacKay, sir.'

'Do you tell me? . . . Daniel MacKay.' Donald wrote down the name. 'Will you be any relation to the two MacKays who came in ahead of you?'

'Nosir. No relation, sir.'

'And what kind of a chob would yours be?'

'Corksuckersir.'

Donald jumped to his feet. Puce in the face and eye grim, he thundered, 'It's the gless-house for you if you dare to play a game with me. I'll double-march you on that quay till you swim in your sweat. . . . Now, think again. What iss your chob?'

'Corksuckersir.'

'Spell it!' snapped Donald, and shot the man a look to hole a battleship.

'C-o-r-k-s-u-c-k-e-r, sir.'

Donald breathed quick and heavy through his nose. 'So, it iss a cork sucker you are, inteed?'

'Yessir, that's me, sir.'

Donald sank back in his chair. 'You suck corks for a liffing? Chust that!' He was purring like a tiger. 'In my infinite mercy I said you'd swim in your sweat. I'll see to it now you drown—unless you can explain to my entire satisfaction. Go ahead. What is a cork sucker?'

'Sir, I worked in a bottle factory. Every day empty bottles came back from the shops in crates. My job was to look over the empties, and extract any corks pushed inside. I used a machine to suck them out by vacuum. I'm a corksuckersir.'

Donald was dumbfounded. His face went expressionless. 'Well, yess, now, inteed. So, it iss a cork sucker you

99

are.' He took down all the particulars and sent the man away.

'Next man!' cried the petty officer.

The fourth marched in. Tall, dark, and saturnine, he held himself straight. His eye held a fire to match even Donald's.

'Name?' barked Donald, and leaning his chest on the desk stabbed a forefinger at him like a dirk: 'Do not be telling me your name iss MacKay.'

'That iss a strange thing to say to me, sir. . . . The truth iss that my name *iss* MacKay! Euan MacKay.'

'Merciful heaven!' cried Donald. He jumped up and sat down. 'I haff had in here a Jock MacKay, an Aeneas MacKay, and a Daniel MacKay—one a sock tucker, one a coke sacker, one a cork sucker.'

'Oich, oich!' exclaimed MacKay. 'But iss that not bad! Pay no heed to them, sir. Chust pretenders they are. Chust pretenders.'

'Indeed, iss that so!' Donald leaned across the desk and shouted, 'Tell me, then—what kind of a MacKay are you?'

Proudly Euan drew himself up. 'Me, sir? Haff no doubt of me, sir. I am the Real MacKay.'

It was he who now has Liabaig Inn. So there you have it. That is how a pot still came to be set in the cave of Coire Garbh. A MacAoidh of MacAoidh, distiller of *uisque beatha*, was the agent sent by divine providence.

WULLIE THE POST

10

ONE thing that Iain Munro at the Screavie store could never sell was paper-backs and magazines. Life around Loch Screavie held more drama than printed paper. Folk could hear their fill of it on their own doorsteps, so long as Wullie the postman was going his rounds. 'The creatt gossip is Wullie,' all people agreed. 'The long ears and sherp eyes has he: there iss nothing effer slips by him.' Still and all, he was no Jeremiah. If there was a light side to the darkest tale, Wullie could see it. His unrelenting optimism could often be exasperating, and as hard to bear as melancholia. In a born story-teller like Wullie, this was a disease, for the teeth were drawn from scandal, and what hope could there be for a good climax to disaster when he always ended, 'Och, it could haff been worse'?

When he was telling of the latest affairs of the young Earl of Ewe, and folk taking the trouble to cast up their eyes pious-like and to say scandalized, 'Earl or no, the Lord will roast him in the Pit for this,' Wullie's 'It could haff been worse,' was irritating enough, but the kirk-elders were black-affronted when he said the same on the capsizing into Loch Screavie of old Jacob's coffin, corpse and all.

One December night in the bar of Screavie Inn, some of the men were discussing the symptoms of Wullie's disease, and seeking a possible cure. Niall Cameron the policeman was there, and Sandy MacTavish, and Black Erchie, and Jamie, the Earl's head-keeper. Outside were steely stars and iron frost, and inside a fire to blister the paint off the walls. Meg Chisholm was serving at the bar.

'There is chust no cure for Wullie,' said Erchie. 'It iss me that has taxed him with it, and aalways he has an answer.'

'There iss some folk would call it a virtue,' suggested Meg, supporting her breasts on the bar and parting the hair from her eyes with her fingers, 'to be seeing the silver lining in the darkest deeds.'

'Och,' said Niall, 'every virtue has a limit, after which it iss a vice. It iss the dark deeds of Screavie that keep you all happy. It would be a dull life with no bit scandal to keep us going.'

'Chust that!' said Sandy. 'Wullie comes his rounds cheering us up, and no one else can do it like him. He will haff us roused near to ecstasy, then dash the gless from our lips with that tailpiece. A real affliction it iss, and a way must be found to stop it.'

'It iss you that hass small cause for complaint, Sandy,' remarked Jamie Urquhart. 'When the tinker's skeleton wass found in the Screavie burn, and we aal thought it yours, Wullie was surely right when he said, "It could haff been worse." '

Sandy bristled. 'Did you ask him on what grounds?'

'I did. Said he to me, "Sandy enjoys more peace as a corp than a husband and Flo makes a better widow than wife." '

Loud and long was the laugh at this, for the reply was double-edged: first, it spoke truth, and second, Wullie had spent many a happy hour with Flo in these days and Sandy not knowing it.

'Chust that!' said Sandy. 'Wullie iss a wit, I can see. He came near to spoiling the best day of my life when Fhairson wass hangit. I had been looking forward to that morning for many a week. On my way to Inverness to celebrate I met Wullie at Garve, and says he to me, "It could haff been worse."

' "You tell me how that could be," I challenged him. "He iss to be hangit by the neck until he iss dead for a murder he confessed committing."

' "Och," says Wullie, "he could haff been hangit for a murder he did not commit."

'True it wass too, and something of the pleasure I had in the event wass taken from me.'

'There must be a way to caw the legs from under him,' insisted Jamie. 'In a place like Screavie, which iss not civilized like the big cities down south, it iss chust a matter of time till something happens that could *not* be worse. Then we haff him!'

'Aye, that will be the day!' agreed Niall. 'But will any of us be here to see it?'

'Something should be done to hasten the day,' suggested Jamie. 'It iss hard to be patient, with Wullie still living in the midst of us.'

'Now, what would you mean by that?' asked Sandy eagerly.

'He means we could lay a trap,' said Niall, who was quick in the uptake, being a policeman.

'What kind of a trap?' asked Erchie sceptically.

'An idea has chust passed through my mind,' announced Niall, giving the others a wink. 'But effery idea must be given a wee bit time to germinate. We must wait till Wullie hass a day off, and iss away from the village, then maybe the creatt scandal will come to pass, and when we tell it, even he will be silenced.'

'Och, I will wager you cannot catch Wullie that way!' swore Erchie. 'It will fail—aalways he has an answer—I will wager you aal a bottle of Talisker.'

'Done!' cried Niall. He explained what he had in mind and Erchie when he heard tried to withdraw from his bet. Aye, but they held him to it: he could well afford it, and that Talisker looked as good as won.

Niall's plan was a masterpiece, for the root of it was a bit of scandal uncovered by Wullie himself. Fiona of Glen Buie—she of the hair black as the raven's wing, and the skin like spring snow, and the cheeks of her red as rowan-berries in September—had been married three years to Iain Munro who kept the store. They had a house by the Screavie burn at the far end of the village. But the marriage had fast gone on the rocks. Iain lived on his nerves and had a terrible temper. Whatever he did was done in haste—even inside his shop he moved at the double—and he was always rushing off to Inverness to fetch this or that bit of goods that could well have waited till next week. He was efficient, but wearing to live with. Fiona was the opposite. A languor-ous lass, she dearly loved her bed and a man to warm it. Fiona could put life in a nutshell—to her it meant love. In that respect her mind was too practical, and some would have said confined to a rut. Iain's motto, 'Late to bed and early to rise,' reckoned hours between sheets as time lost. Since Fiona was of quite opposite mind, and since Iain was so often away on his overnight jaunts to Inverness, she began to have young Hamish Stewart the forester in to keep her company.

Wullie the post, who was early awheel to run the mail to Garve, would sometimes see Hamish at six in the morning, heading back to the village from the house by the Screavie burn. Fiona might have other nocturnal visitors, hinted Wullie, but never could he put a name to them, 'which means,' he added, 'they must be smert, smert.' Young Dougal MacFarlane was thought of, even Euan MacKay, but that was just gossip, since folk were tantalised.

A week or two later, at Hogmanay, the conspirators had gathered in Meg Chisholm's bar when Niall arrived and took them aside. Said he, 'The time has come. Wullie the post went off early this afternoon to veesit relations at Ullapool. It iss him will be back on New Year's night and straight into Meg's bar to hear what gossip he's missed. We must aal be here—and Erchie with the money to stand us the Talisker.'

It was agreed. On New Year's night there was a ceilidh and dance at the village hall, and few at Meg's bar save Niall, Black Erchie, Sandy, and Jamie. That Wullie would come first to Meg's to prime himself they were certain, but when nine o'clock came and still no Wullie they began to feel uneasy.

A few minutes later he was at the door, broad and beefy, and his face shining like a beacon. 'Happy New Year!' cried he, and came to shake hands. He looked around, startled. 'Why, you look awfu' glum, Erchie, and you Niall —the whole lot of yous! Funereal faces on the first day of the year! What in the Name hass taken you?'

It was heads not hands they shook. As a token of esteem, and after a judicious pause, Niall alone took his hand, and fixing his gaze sorrowfully on the floor, said, 'Aye, you mean well, Wullie, and glad we are to see you back. But this iss not the time or place for laughter and chollity.'

'Indeed, no,' Jamie bore him out, 'this day will go down in the history books of Screavie ass the Day of Calamity.'

' "Cry, Havoc! and let slip the togs," ' intoned Sandy. 'Aal iss calamity and us here chust to be fortifying our speerits, and to steady our nerves after the shocks.'

Wullie was now like a hen on a hot girdle, and jumping from foot to foot. 'What hass happened?' he pleaded. . . . 'And me away when it did!' he moaned.

'A terrible drama it iss,' said Niall, 'and for me the busiest day I haff had in the poliss. Ass like ass not the Glasgow C.I.D. will be up to investigate.'

'The Glasgow C.I.D.!' exclaimed Wullie, his eyes alight with excitement. 'Hass a body been killed?'

'Did you not see the smoking ruins on your way into the village?' asked Jamie.

'Och, it wass a fire?' guessed Wullie. 'The night wass pitch black and the road icy. It wass not me looked aside.'

'It wass not chust a fire,' Niall assured him. 'That wass the least of it. The trouble started when Iain Munro went off to Inverness for Hogmanay, and Fiona wass left to herself.'

'Man, I can see the way of it now,' interrupted Wullie. 'That young villain Hamish Stewart would be in for the night.'

'Right you are,' said Niall. 'But what Fiona and Hamish neffer knew wass that Iain Munro's car broke down at Garve. A bad leak it took in the radiator, and not a garage open. He stopped at the hotel to see in the New Year, then came straight back, topping up his radiator at the burns. Hours it took him, but he was back at five in the morning.'

'Cot bless my soul!' exclaimed Wullie. 'Hamish neffer leaves till near six. So he caught him then?'

'Red-handed. Opened the front door of the house and there wass Hamish in his gallowses, coming out of the bathroom tooth-brush in hand.'

'Och, then' began Wullie, 'it could haff been—'

'Stop you!' cried Niall. 'Iain went mad when he saw. Maybe there wass still a bit dram in him. He ran to the wall and seized his gun. Hamish did not wait to argue. He streaked to the front door and out—too late. Aye, before he could lay hand on the garden gate, Iain shot him dead.'

Wullie paled. 'Chust that! Shot in his tracks, like a

grouse on the twelfth and this not even August! The unlucky lad, aye, the poor sowl that he iss. He hass been
changed. He will not be enchoying his Hogmanays where
he iss now. . . . Still and aal, it could haff been—'

'Stop you!' said Niall. 'Iain wass now berserk. Said he to
himself, mostlike, "I may ass well be hanged for a sheep ass
a lamb," for in he runs to the bedroom with the smoking
gun in his hand, and without so much ass a by-your-leave
he shoots Fiona dead in her bed.'

Wullie was thunder-struck. Erchie was watching with
bated breath, scarcely believing his man could rally after
that stroke. 'And me away at Ullapool!' bewailed Wullie at
last, 'and missing the trachedy of the century! . . . Yess,
indeed, poor Fiona, the poor sowl that she iss. So, she hass
been changed too, like Hamish. She hass been reaped with
him and will sin no more. . . . There iss aye this to be said,
it could haff been—'

'Stop you!' cried Niall. 'When Iain sees what he has done,
he decides, in cold blood now, and with aal premeditaation,
to make a proper chob of this New Year morn. He scatters
petrol around the floors and furniture and sets a light to it.
In a few meenutes the house vanishes from sight in a sea of
flames, and before anyone at Screavie knew, it wass burnt
to the ground.'

Wullie was dumbfoundered. All save Erchie were
scanning him confidently, sure now that this had him beaten.
Erchie was downcast.

Wullie found his tongue. 'It iss the Fall of the House of
Munro. The old grey house by the Screavie burn. Many's
the Christmas parcel I deliffered there, and the unpaid
bills I collected. Aal gone. Chust cinders and ashes. It iss
a sad tale that iss in it. Aye, if only stones could speak—and
if they could, they would say as I say, "It could haff been—"'

'Stop you!' cried Niall, 'for the trachedy iss not ended.

107

When Iain sees the house go up in flames, he waits till aal inside iss a raching furnace, and then walks straight in to perish, aye, into the very hert of that inferno—to be roasted alive.'

Wullie was aghast. Nearly grey in the face instead of his usual beetroot, he bent his head in meditation. Niall had given his knock-out blow. The men were thirsting for the Talisker. Then Wullie spoken solemn. 'It iss a lesson for us aal,' said he: 'a wife needs more of a man than cot and fodder, and to keep her well content is canny work. Else murder, arson, and suicide can be the end. Chust that! Screavie has aye been a stage for drama, but this one might be straight from Shakespeare's own pen. No wonder you stood ass grave ass undertakers when I came in the door! Wayward iss the decrees of fate that on this day of aal days I should be absent. But aal things conseedered, and when aal has been said and done—it could haff been worse.'

Niall gave a cry of fury. 'Worse? Fiona seduced, three folk dead, one roasted alive, not one survivor and the house a burnt-out shell! *How could* it haff been worse, tell me that?'

'If Iain Munro had come back the night before,' said Wullie, 'the man he shot would haff been me.'

FOR BETTER FOR WORSE?

11

When Erchie MacFarlane flitted to Screavie House, great was the talk at Screavie village. It was not just the inheritance of old Jacob's money and the move from a croft to a big house that made the stir, but that Catriona was living there too. 'You haff to be a Lord Ewe to get away with the likes of that,' said some, 'not chust a fusherman.' Folk were scandalised. They knew nothing of the terms of old Jacob's will, which forbade Erchie to marry. Only the minister, and the Earl of Ewe and his lady, knew anything of that, and though they shook their heads they said never a word.

Erchie and Catriona were very much in love. All went well that first year: never did you see a more devoted pair. Then one day Erchie says, 'Catriona, it iss an anxious look I sometimes see in your eye. It comes and goes when you look at me and think I am not noticing. Tell me, lass, what iss in your mind?'

'Och,' says she, 'it iss nothing at aal. You are imachining.'

'Could it be,' suggested Erchie, 'that you are thinking this iss too good to last and that you are not marrit?'

Catriona was startled and embarrassed too. 'Indeed, yess,' she acknowledged, 'such a thought has passed through my mind. But there iss no help for that. We must chust forget aal about it.'

'It will not let you forget,' declared Erchie, 'if it iss the feeling of insecurity you haff. We must get marrit soon.'

'But how could we do that?' gasped Catriona. 'You would lose aal Jacob's money. It would go to his grand-nephew, the Earl of Ewe.'

'There iss more than one answer to that, I am thinking. The first iss that our love means more to me than money. The second iss that we can marry, yet haff the money too. Where there's a wull there's a way: it wass you taught me that, Catriona.'

'Spin me no riddles, Erchie MacFarlane. We cannot marry and not haff it rechistered. No one would do it: so what do you mean?'

'Undone we would be,' agreed Erchie, 'if it wass rechistered. But stop you! Tell me this: provided you were married by a meenister and it not rechistered, would you not feel bound chust as strongly as if it *wass* rechistered? Would you not?'

'Indeed, yess,' Catriona said. 'Rechistration iss chust a formality.'

'The same for me,' declared Erchie. 'The vow would bind me.'

'Doctor MacLeod would neffer agree to that,' protested Catriona. 'Evading the law of the land!'

'It wass not the Reverend Doctor I had in mind,' said Erchie in a small voice: 'it wass the meenister before him— the Reverend Alasdair MacColl. He lives alone in a cottage near Dundonnell. Eighty-eight he iss if a day, and long retired. It wass he baptized me, and would marry me too if I asked him.'

'You mean he iss not in his right mind?' asked Catriona.

'Och, it would be going too far to say that: chust say a wee bit wandered. He has the Gaelic and not much English. His eyesight iss bad and the time he will live short. I will know how to manache him—if you will be letting me veesit him at Dundonnell.'

Catriona threw herself in his arms with joy, for there was nothing she wanted so much as to be married. Next morning, Erchie went off to Dundonnell and saw the Reverend Alasdair. Now, that was a real preacher in his day, broad and hairy like a Highland ox, with a pulpit bellow that echoed round the hills like the clap of doom. Frail and tottery as he was now, he still made a fine figure of a man with his white beard, which had not been cut for sixty years save for trimmings at the fringe.

'Cot bless my soul!' cried he in the Gaelic when Erchie found him in his garden. 'I will be knowing your face well. It iss Mr MacKenzie you are?'

'Not MacKenzie—MacFarlane. Erchie MacFarlane.'

'Well now, here I am thinking to myself aal these years it was Mr MacKenzie I met,' said he, airing his English, 'when what I met wass a mistake.'

Erchie reminded him of the MacFarlanes of Ullapool, and soon the old man was beginning to recall details—births, deaths, baptisms, and marriages. 'It iss a wife I now haff,' said Erchie, 'but we haff neffer been marrit by a meenister, and you it iss we would like to perform the service, who wass after marrying my own father.'

The Reverend Alasdair beamed with pleasure. 'But stop you!' said he, 'I haff no kirk and cannot do it.' Erchie replied that aal he and Catriona wanted was a private service in the minister's own house and no one else present. 'It iss not the formalities we haff to bother with now,' said he, 'but to sanctify what iss aalready done.'

'Chust that! Iss it not the heathen savage you are, Erchie MacFarlane! But I would not be leaving the lass unwedded. . . . I suppose you will haff a wee bit of a certeeficate to show me?'

'Here it iss,' said Erchie, passing over a copy of his father's marriage certificate.

The Reverend Alasdair scarcely gave it a glance. Why try to read English print when it was there to see, and himself with bad eyes? 'Well, then,' he consented, 'since it iss not the banns you want called, nor psalms sung, but the solemnisation of matrimony, bring you the lass as soon as she iss willing.'

Late one evening next week, Erchie and Catriona were married in the cottage at Dundonnell. Not a soul saw them, not a line was ever sent to a registrar, and twelve months had barely gone before old Alasdair was dead.

Shuna, the Countess of Ewe, was every bit as happy in Castle Ross as Catriona in Screavie House. But Simon, the Earl, was not as happy as Erchie. Shuna had two fine boys and Simon still loved her. His trouble was money. He had overspent on putting the estate in order, then had lost money in a business venture in London. At breakfast one morning he was sharing his troubles with Shuna.

'It's a great pity,' said she, 'that Archie and Catriona have been unable to marry. Village gossip has it that in fact they *are* married. I discount that, of course, yet I wonder— might they not marry? They are west highlanders.'

Simon regarded her with astonishment. 'Daft as west highlanders sometimes are, Shuna, they're not that daft. I should know. I was born here.'

'I mean that the people have strong traditions, which give them a very high code of behaviour—oh, don't look at me like that, Simon, as if to whisper "illicit stills and illegitimates"—these are exceptions to a rule. Codes and traditions fail if you thwart men's natural instincts too long, but they give them up uneasily. Now, take Catriona: a lively West Highland lass, richer than us. She'd want to marry Archie. How long would he last out, do you think, just for the sake of the money?'

Simon pondered, and the more he thought the brighter and more hopeful grew the light in his eye. 'Shuna, the village folk could be right. Archie MacFarlane is no timid man. He's a born buccaneer. I think I'll pay a visit to Screavie House—just to look around and see what I can see.'

'Don't give them advance warning,' counselled Shuna. 'Just drop in.'

The Earl of Ewe called at Screavie House on a fine summer evening. 'I want to wish you well now that you've settled in,' he announced, cheerfully ignoring that Erchie and Catriona had been living two and a half years in the house. A full hour he stayed, and a fine crack they all had. They plied him first with tea, then liked him well enough for Erchie to get out his Glenlivet. The longer he stayed the more they took to him, and he to them. When he left, Erchie saw him off at the front door then hastened back to Catriona, saying 'I wonder, now, what brought *him* here?'

Catriona was sitting up alert. 'He has heard,' said she, 'or has guessed. No man will keep a cat-like interest through an hour unless he has suspeecions. He wass trying to see efferything and to miss nothing. If his wife had come in his place I might haff taken fright. Och, but he iss chust a man! You did fine, Erchie: you deceived him and so did I.'

'It iss old Alasdair I am thinking of: might he not haff talked before he died?'

'Where would be the effidence? Would he effer talk to anyone the Earl would meet?'

The pair of them felt safe and happy, as well they might had they heard Lord Ewe that night. 'It's no use, Shuna,' said he over the dinner table. 'They're not married. Archie's eyes hardly left her face save when he spoke to me; as for her, she hung on every word he said. These two are a pair of lovers, no more.'

Shuna felt a pang of disappointment. 'It does sound conclusive. But maybe Catriona's a clever woman. Knowing how unobservant you are, my dear, I refuse to be downcast. Could there not be something you missed? For example, did Catriona ever leave the room? If so, why?'

'Several times. Wait till I think. She went to fetch tea things, and later the whisky and glasses.'

'So! Archie sat there and let her do it all?—made no move even to bring the drinks! Yet the West Highlander is better-mannered than a townsman. Tell me, did he rise to open the door, when she either came or went?'

'No, I'm afraid not.'

'There's hope, Simon! He takes her for granted. Before marriage, only an ass does that.'

'My God, Shuna, the sweat begins to break on my brow!'

'Oh, I know—you are no better than he. Still, let's concentrate on Screavie House. Had he to render himself any service, when she might have helped him?'

'He had rubber boots on when I came, and we'd been sitting a short time when he began to wonder where his slippers were, and had to rise to fetch them.'

'A small point, in itself. Still, it all adds up. What was her hair like?'

'How d'you mean, Shuna? It's the most wonderful golden colour, of course; the sheen on it's like early morning sun on the sea.'

'I mean tidy or untidy.' Her voice was short.

'Oh, it was certainly a bit of a mess, as if she'd been out in the wind—but she suits it marvellously well that way.'

'Suit it or not, by the late afternoon an unmarried girl will want a style better than a "bit of a mess." Yes, Simon, this line of inquiry is worth following up. I'll do some detective work of my own in the village.'

'And I'll have records searched. . . .'

A thorough search of the records was soon made by the Registrar General at Edinburgh, and when that showed nothing, at Somerset House in London. It seemed that Erchie and Catriona were not married. 'It's no use, Shuna,' repeated Simon one night, showing her the letters from the registrars. 'A couple can't even be married abroad and escape registration in the U.K. They're living in sin at Screavie House, and that's that.'

Shuna was still not convinced. 'It takes more than registrars to beat a clever woman. I've been having a talk with Janet Dunbar, and have checked what she told me with others at Screavie. Archie is over at the pub not just once a week but four nights in seven. What man will leave his woman that often unless marriage has made him sure of her?—or unless he wants rid of her, and there's no suggestion that Archie isn't on good terms with Catriona.'

The Countess had discovered too that when Erchie was away on business at Inverness, or Kyle, he would stop on his way home at nights to visit his old friends at Screavie— Niall Cameron the policeman, or Donald MacPherson, or Sandy MacTavish—indeed, many an hour he delayed by the wayside before going on to Screavie House. Never a thought did folk give to that, but the Countess gave it thought. 'It doesn't add up to proof,' said she to Simon, 'but I feel convinced myself that Archie and Catriona have taken the marriage vow. They'll grow careless still more as time goes on. Let's give them another month or two to feel safe.'

On hearing all this, Lord Ewe had a notion of his own. One day when he was at the manse discussing the kirk with the reverend doctor, and hearing that each year Erchie was giving a thousand pounds to the kirk funds, he asked, 'Has Archie any friends in the ministry? Does any minister other than you call on him?'

'Not that effer I heard,' said Doctor MacLeod. 'It iss

most unlikely. Why would you be asking that?'

'Sorry, I'm not free to say, yet I've urgent reasons. Does any minister other than you know his family?'

'There was Alasdair MacColl, who meenistered at Ullapool. He came here as he aged, him wanting the smaller kirk. He retired to Dundonnell—died there a year ago. I wass there at the graveside, and so wass Erchie MacFarlane. A sad, sad day, and him with the finest beard that effer was grown in Ross, like the falls of Glomach in spate.'

Next day Lord Ewe drove to Dundonnell, returning at night to confer with his Countess. 'Shuna,' said he 'they were married at Dundonnell by the Reverend Alasdair MacColl.' She jumped to her feet. 'Simon! You have proof? How do you know?'

He told her all. The postman at Dundonnell distinctly remembered that one day when he called with the daily newspaper about a year before Alasdair died, the old man had told him that he had married a couple of former parishioners the previous night.

'He heard the names?' insisted Shuna, 'or where they came from?'

'Neither. I've tried the nearest shop, manse, hotel—no one else had heard the story. There's no proof. But marriage by night is unusual to say the least, and who would want it so much as Archie and Catriona? I want you to invite them to dinner. We'll have a chance to observe closely, and if we see justification I'll deal with Archie before he goes home.'

'We can do better than dine them here,' said Shuna. 'Johnnie Drumgast rang me today. He invites us over next Friday for dinner. I accepted. He asked was there anyone else we'd specially like to meet. I said no, I'd leave it to him. Simon, why not ring up and say you'd like the MacFarlanes? They'd be much less on their guard there than here. Suggest too that he ask that new Robertson woman from Liabaig.'

Simon went straight to the telephone. In a few minutes it was arranged.

When the invitation came to Screavie House, Catriona felt surprised and flattered, but the happy thought that here was the chance to wear her new evening dress from Edinburgh obliterated every other reflection. Erchie was pleased too, at this acknowledgement of Catriona's position—he never gave tuppence for his own. They arrived at Drumgast's house on Friday at a carefully timed five minutes past the hour. The Ewes had come early and were out on the terrace to watch. Erchie stepped out of his car, and the first thing the Countess noted was that he made no move to open the passenger's door for Catriona. She had to scramble out unaided.

'Almost certainly married,' whispered Shuna to Simon.

They all went indoors. Besides the MacFarlanes and Ewes, the party included the Reverend Dr MacLeod and Mrs MacLeod, and Mrs Robertson of Liabaig—her hair bleached as white as the quartzite screes of Beinn Eighe, yet only twenty-five and a widow, her figure straight as a hazel-wand and her eye-shadow green as a hill-corrie. Erchie could hardly keep his eyes off her. He had seen nothing like this in his life and made straight to her. Soon they were in conversation. The Countess noted this with satisfaction. If Erchie was unmarried, he would take Catriona in to dinner and sit beside her; if married, he would most naturally take Mrs Robertson.

'What do you think now?' whispered Simon to Shuna. 'Too soon to be sure,' she answered. 'Catriona must have paid a hundred and twenty pounds for that dress she's wearing, yet the fit isn't perfect—she's allowed herself to put on weight. I think she's married.'

In the twenty minutes that followed, not once did Erchie and Catriona seek each other out to speak, and the eyes of the Countess were gleaming like those of a lioness before tethered lambs. When dinner was served, Drumgast led in Lady Ewe, and Lord Ewe quickly took Mrs MacLeod. The move had been planned to leave Erchie a straight choice: Catriona or Mrs Robertson. The Reverend MacLeod, warned in advance, hung back to see how the dice would fall. Erchie walked headlong into the trap. He and Mrs Robertson sauntered side by side into the dining-room, and the Reverend Doctor paired with Catriona.

That dinner went well, for the Ewes were in sparkling form, eyes dancing and hearts light. But for all her wit, the Countess never took her eyes off the mark: she saw a dozen little things that escaped everyone else—how Erchie was no longer watching Catriona with the constantly admiring eyes of a year ago, nor she hanging on his words, for scant attention she paid; how they sat opposite across the table yet failed to serve each other for all the attention bestowed on their partners; how she contradicted him sharply when he swore that the greatest of all callings was the sea and ships. As soon as dinner was over Shuna beckoned Simon aside and said: 'They are married. There's no room for doubt— the Dundonnell story is true. Go in for the kill.'

Lord Ewe spoke to Drumgast, and a couple of hours later he drew Erchie aside. 'Mr MacFarlane, before we leave I'd like a word with you in private. Would you come with me now to Sir John's study? I've asked him for the use of it.' Surprised as he was, Erchie assented. They went through to the study and seated themselves on either side of Sir John's desk. Sir John had left a bottle of Strath Isla there, with two glasses and a scribbled note: *Drink up!* They laughed and helped themselves. 'A thoughtful man iss Chonnie,' remarked Erchie. 'Now sir, what did you want to say?'

Lord Ewe gave Erchie one of his most disarming smiles.

'I have been seeking in my own mind,' said he, 'for the best way to do you a service.'

'Man!' exclaimed Erchie, 'that iss right kind of you. It iss not me that iss in need of any service, so far ass I know.'

'No?' The Earl raised a quizzical eyebrow and smiled again. 'If not you, Catriona, then—it is hard not to think of you two as one. No, no, don't protest: your devotion is apparent, my dear fellow. It's utterly wrong that you should have to live a bachelor, she a spinster, because of those monstrous terms in my grand-uncle's will. He had no understanding of men and women, believing all to be like himself, or else that so they should be. Ironically, he was a man of good heart: he didn't really imagine money to be any substitute for happiness, yet went and imposed that substitution on you and Catriona. You live alone at Screavie House. It's a big place. It needs a family to bring it alive. I'm quite sure old Jacob wanted your happiness, and that makes me sure you should marry Catriona and damn the will.'

Erchie grinned. 'True it iss, I like Catriona fine. I agree with some of what you say, but I am not the man to throw away four hundred thousand pounds.'

'You need not throw it away, Mr MacFarlane.'

Erchie gave him a sharp look. 'What do you mean by that, my lord. A wull iss a wull.'

'The will says that if you marry a tenth goes to the church and the rest to me. If you are willing to marry, I would relinquish in your favour a part of what's due me: in other words, I'd be willing to give you a share.'

'Would you indeed, my lord. It iss kind of you to think of me, and I must give you a plain answer: I'll not accept.'

'Mr MacFarlane, I want to be generous. The last thing I wish to do is to pitchfork you back into your old life. That would be cruel and stupid, and I'm not a cruel or stupid man. I'd rather go without some of the money, and beg you not to reject the solution I've offered. If you do, the law might force me to take all.'

Erchie felt a pang of alarm and stiffened. The Earl took note: the light in Erchie's eye was neither anger nor puzzlement, but alarm. The puzzled eye switched on a second later, a conscious act. The hook has struck, thought the Earl, and the fish a fighter—if I reel in too quick he'll snap the gut and away.

'I don't follow your lordship,' said Erchie. 'What do you mean by "law" and "force"?'

The Earl raised his glass. 'A toast!' said he, and stood. 'I drink to the bonniest wife in Ross: Mrs Catriona MacFarlane of Screavie House.' He emptied the glass and sat down, staring Erchie in the eye, but with a most friendly expression.

'She would like to be that!' commented Erchie. 'No doubt of it. Och, but it cannot be! We must chust put temptaation behind us—not talk of it more.'

'I'm not suggesting she'd *like* to be,' said the Earl. 'I'm suggesting she is. At Dundonnell two years ago, was it not? Wise man. Does you credit.'

Erchie turned white. 'Chust that! Cot bless my soul! How did you come to hear of that—that flight of fancy?'

'You admit the truth of it, then?'

'I do not! Maleecious gossip! Maleecious! Who could be up to people! Can you be telling me who spun you that fairy-tale?'

'I'm sure that you yourself, Mr MacFarlane, would not be doubting the word of the Reverend Alasdair MacColl.'

'Not when he wass in full possession of his faculties. In his last years he wass chust a wandered old man.'

'You knew him, then? Mr MacFarlane, your secret is out. I know you for an honest man, and that you'll not now have the heart to maintain a pretence. For my part, I've no heart to plunder you. I'd like you and Catriona to enjoy your riches in peace, free of anxieties, with a quiet mind and good conscience in all future years. I'm ready to forget what I know. On the other hand, I mustn't forget I'm a father. My estate was long neglected, and has lately cost me more than I bargained for. When my children grow up, must they damn me for weakness because I failed to claim at least some part of what is due me under Jacob's will? No. I will not betray their interest. A harder man that I would lay proofs before you then go to the courts and seize all. I prefer to keep silent, to respect the new life that you and Catriona have made for yourselves, yet to entreat your own generosity in return for mine.'

'What iss this proposal?' asked Erchie gruffly. His mind was in a whirl. No man likes a tooth drawn, though the sacrifice be for health's sake. The Earl seemed to know the whole story. If the truth was spread around Screavie, how could he and Catriona keep the money and ever look folk in the eye? Maybe he could himself, but Catriona? No.

The Earl took from his pocket two documents. 'One of these papers,' said he, 'should be signed by you and the other by me. My one forfeits half of what I would receive from Jacob Frewin's trustees if you marry, and undertakes to return it to you. Your paper applies only if you choose not to declare a marriage. It agrees to pay me one half of what you received from the trustees both now by way of annual dividends and later by way of capital sums. By our signing both you have free choice of action.' He presented his fountain pen to Erchie.

Erchie pushed the pen aside. His panic had vanished. Here was Ewe offering two hundred thousand pounds! He would not be as generous as that, thought Erchie, if his evidence could stand the light of day. The instinct to drive a hard bargain revived. 'Now iss this not the creatt tale you haff told me!' smiled he. 'I must be asking you to show me your proofs. Without proofs, who would believe a tissue of lies like that?'

'I think plenty of people would believe it,' sighed Lord Ewe, 'but I'm sure you and I don't want them even to hear of it. Gossip is so quickly believed true in Screavie. No, it's the Court of Chancery that will ask for proofs, which can't be given to you now, but must go to them. This means you will shortly hear from the Lord Chancellor.'

'The Lord Chancellor!' exclaimed Erchie, dismayed. 'He would summon me before a court?'

'There could be no choice. You will be required to testify under oath, and then be cross-examined by counsel. Of course, if the evidence against you is untrue, then all's well—and the money yours to enjoy.'

'Chust that! Pass me that document you haff. I will be signing it for the sake of your children, to save aal this trouble you would be haffing—if you will sign yours.'

They each signed and exchanged contracts. After brief expressions of friendship they returned to the drawing-room where the party soon broke up. The moment Catriona had Erchie outside in the car she burst out, 'Erchie, has something happened? What did he want you for? Has he heard?'

'It iss bad news I haff, Catriona—someone has given us away. Old Alasdair betrayed us.' He told her all that had passed between him and Lord Ewe.

'Deception!' cried Catriona. 'Chust deception! Nothing was signed at Dundonnel. Alasdair is dead. There iss no legal evidence whateffer—aal would be hearsay, and the meenister himself a wandered old soul, dreaming of bygone days. Erchie, aal you had to do was to sit tight. The Earl could not haff made a move.'

Erchie protested, but the more he justified himself the

angrier Catriona grew. The argument went on long after they were home in bed, and next morning she announced, 'This very evening I am off to see his lordship. Would you give me that signed paper if you please?' For the sake of peace, Erchie held his tongue. He gave her the paper and said he would go out with her to give support. But no, she would have none of that. 'This iss a chob for a wuman,' said she. 'There iss one fool in effery married couple, and this no time to let him loose. If you will chust be keeping calm and quiet at home I will see the Earl myself.'

She rang up Castle Ross at five o'clock to be sure Lord Ewe was at home, and was there at six. He met her at the great doorway and led her into the hall. 'My dear Catriona,' said he, 'how delightful to have a call from you! Please come to the sitting-room and meet Shuna.'

'Business before pleasure, my lord. Here iss the wee bit paper you gave Erchie last night. He wants back the one he gave you in exchange, and here iss me to fetch it.'

'If he wants it back he must have it,' agreed Lord Ewe. 'Does he give a reason?'

'He and I may live at Screavie House,' said Catriona, 'but as far as you and the law are concerned we are not marrit.'

'Indeed? How happy we should all be if you were! Now before we say more, please come and have a drink with Shuna and me, then we'll let you go. . . . No, no, I do insist— it's not everyday we have so welcome a visitor. Let us do all we have to do in the friendliest spirit.'

Despite herself, Catriona felt Simon's charm wrap her round. She was most relieved too to find no trace of hostility. So in she went to a spacious yet comfortable sitting-room, panelled in light oak, the tables littered with magazines, books, and papers, and the Countess playing with her elder son on the hearth-rug before a blazing fire. They shook hands and talked while Lord Ewe decanted and served the sherry. The boy Nigel, aged two, was playing with wooden bricks. Catriona had just said a few words praising Nigel's strong limbs and ruddy face when he, finding himself neglected by his mother, threw a brick at his father. It smashed the crystal glass in his hand. Lord Ewe threw the fragments in the fire and calmly drew a new glass from a cabinet. 'Shuna,' said he, 'that wretched boy should have been in bed an hour ago.'

'He is not "that wretched boy," ' she rebuked him. 'Nigel's bed-time is six-thirty.' His lip tightened: 'Always after five his temper grows short. I think it a sure sign.' Her eye was icy: 'Simon, leave it to me to decide his bed-time, if you please.'

Lord Ewe said nothing, but Catriona could see from his face that he would have more to say later, both to Shuna and son. Meantime, he began to explain to Catriona his plan to reafforest the hillside above Screavie House, and his wish to confer with Erchie. The Countess was listening politely, but Catriona saw that twice she swallowed yawns before rising to put Nigel to bed.

Lord Ewe and Catriona remained a few minutes together. 'We haff still to exchange papers,' she demanded.

'I have your husband's in the writing desk there. You'll have it at once.' He rose and took the paper she offered him, then hesitated. 'I do advise you against this cancellation.'

'You must stop calling him my "husband"—what possible grounds do you haff for such a suspeecion?'

'Come, Catriona, what grounds do you have for suspecting me to be married? . . . Well?'

'I suppose that that iss a rhetorical question? You don't want an answer?'

'Indeed I do. You weren't at my wedding. How can you know I'm really married to Shuna?'

'People told me of the wedding.'

He smiled delightedly. 'You accept that as proof?'

'No, no!' she answered quickly. 'I haff only to come into your house—and at once it iss obvious.'

'Tell me why—suppose you hadn't met Shuna and me before—how would you guess?'

'Oh, by lots of little things. . . . A man and wife are much more easy together—they keep little guard on what they say and do—more familiar, we call it—sometimes they will even bicker over a boy's bed-time.'

'You could not have put it better, Catriona. Passion comes like a whirlwind, and like every good guest doesn't overstay his welcome. Man and wife grow relaxed though they live together. At breakfast the husband can be lost in thought and not even hear his wife speak. She often pays scant attention to his very wisest words. When dining out he is free to leave her in another's company and seek conversation elsewhere.'

'True, too true indeed,' assented Catriona, 'but we are flying off at a tangent.'

'Not at all. We have both described precisely how we know each other to be married. Here in my hand is my signed renunciation of my rightful claim under old Jacob's will. Please take it from me and give it once again to Archie.'

Inwardly agitated, Catriona stood still as stone. 'I want back the contract he signed last night. I promised I would bring it away.'

Lord Ewe gave a groan. 'Then I have to withdraw my own contract, Catriona. I had no wish to break Archie's award under the will, hence sought this way of compromise. But all action now will lie with an impersonal legal machine. Your own conscience, Catriona, will be put to proof under oath by seven judges of the Court of Chancery.'

Catriona stared at him, her eyes gone bleak. She took the

contract from his hand and walked over to the windows and read. Her hand was trembling and she saw nothing—for that matter she knew every word already. A full minute passed in silence. At last she said, 'I will give this bit of paper to Erchie. As soon as banns can be called, he and I will be marrit.'

'You are wise, O Catriona,' said the Earl of Ewe softly, 'because you were wrongly cast in your old part, and will be happier by far in your new—Archie too, for he loves a carefree life. Now he can sing with Omar Khayyam:

"You know, my friend, with what a brave carouse
    I made a second marriage in my house—" '

He accompanied her to the door. Catriona was immensely surprised to find herself all light-heartedness, her troubles shed. 'Erchie will laugh when I come home,' she smiled, 'and have to tell him that *he* wass right.'

'Don't forget to add,' said Lord Ewe, 'that when he talks business or politics and has to watch you stifle a yawn —for you at Screavie House are no different from us at Castle Ross—when he hears you contradict him sharply, when he no longer jumps to open doors at your coming and going, when—but why continue?—he will then know that not only is he married, but that everyone else knows it too.'

Catriona was laughing as he opened the door of her car and bowed her in. 'Straight home with you,' said he. 'Remind Archie that when a man is driving back to his woman, yet stops to chatter with old friends and to dally over a dram at the pub—the whole world knows him a husband.' He gave her a last smile and closed the door.

Two months later, Catriona was married to Erchie at Screavie kirk.

MAIRI

12

MEG's bar was full. Although it was mid-May and the winter past, this was Friday night and even Niall Cameron was there off duty. He had come in with a tale to tell. '*Uisque b'a* for the polissman,' called Erchie, and to Niall, 'How iss crime at Screavie?'

'There iss better than crime afoot here,' declared Niall. 'I wass along the shore-road on my bike last night. Who would you think I met? I will buy aal the Talisker there iss for the man who can guess that . . . I met a mermaid.'

The roar of laughter died away as the door opened on a tall, strong-set young man, his flaming red beard giving him instant recognition—Rhuridh MacAlpine the schoolmaster. A low groan went round the room, for they feared that Niall's story had perished at birth. Rhuridh was here for his weekend mission, and when that happened no man dared broach another subject and stand to the lash of his tongue.

An affliction, that is what religion is when it takes a man as it took Rhuridh MacAlpine. He had not always been this way. Rhuridh was from Lewis, and just twenty-five. A handsomer man you never saw. A coltish grace gave beauty to every move he made, for he was loose of limb, but all that was nothing to his force as a man, which was startling—Rhuridh had personal magneticism, and he could talk as eloquently as an Irishman. When he first came to Screavie the lasses were all a-swoon with excitement. He might have taken his pick. Most of the folk were hoping his choice would fall on Sheila of Liabaig—she of the hair black as a Lewis bog, and her skin smooth like copper birch. She was sister to Morag of Glen Dorcha, and like her as shy with men as Rhuridh with women. Yet as if by instinct the pair had no sooner met than they sought each other out thereafter.

Slow, too slow, was the progress they made that first year and Rhuridh's exaltation could not find a full enough outlet. Marriage might have pains, but celibacy gave him no pleasures. His romantic nature took a wrong turn—wrong, that is, for him. When he took to religion he took to it badly. Before long he was running Sunday school and bible class for the Reverend Doctor MacLeod. It was then that Sheila made a bad mistake. She began attending his advanced bible class every Wednesday night. He was not content just to read the Good Book—he thundered hell-fire and damnation for all the sins of the flesh. He had never been made for a celibate life and trying to live it put him off-balance. He made his teaching sound as if all love between men and women was wicked, except for stock-raising under licence. That was not the real Rhuridh speaking, but after preaching on such a theme he could not be seen walking out with one of his own students, nor be kissing her in the woods by the Screavie burn.

Caught thus in a web of his own weaving, Rhuridh went from bad to worse. He began to call in at Meg's bar on Friday and Saturday nights to convert the village drunks. There were no drunks at Meg's bar. Few could afford a thick night save once in a blue moon. But in Rhuridh's eyes every man who raised glass to lip was lost. 'Wine iss a mocker, strong drink iss raging,' he would cry. 'Whoeffer iss deceived thereby iss not wise.' And he would tell them the tale of woe in the inner furnace of Hell, where 'Deffils with forkit tailies will be driving red-hot pitch-forks into the sinners' powels, till their screams are fanning the flames.' At first Meg's customers listened entranced. They always welcomed diversion. In quick time they wearied and damned Rhuridh as heartily as he damned them—but always with respect, mark you, he being six feet two in his stocking soles, broad in the chest and narrow at the hips, and with a light in his eye. He made life a trial not only for Meg Chisholm and her customers but for all at Screavie. He condemned the dances at the village hall because young men saw lasses home (who could be telling what happened out there in the dark), he denounced the W.R.I. for their raffles, he castigated the Highlands and Islands Film Board for corrupting the young—in short, there was little that man, woman, or bairn could lawfully do in Screavie except take their pews on the Sabbath. In a sense this was high commendation of the man: at Screavie no less a person than Rhuridh could have borne the part, which needed abounding strength and energy.

Out of the corner of an eye, Niall watched Rhuridh walk into the bar, and he made use of the silence to repeat, 'I tell you, it wass a mermaid. It iss not a choke I am telling you.'

Rhuridh usually opened his mission the moment he crossed the threshold, but tonight he stood stock still, for this was the policeman himself, the upholder of law and justice, and if Niall was not what a good Christian policeman should be, still, his office had to be given respect.

'Wass she walking along the road as bold as brass?' asked Erchie, 'or wass her tail tucked underneath her arm?'

Niall looked vexed. 'I wass not on the road. I had left my bike there, and since the night was fine and me needing the exercise, I walked a good mile over the moor to the Cnoc

Ban headland. The moon stood high and near to full and the sea was shining. Standing there at the cliff's edge, I could see the length of the Camus Ban, three miles of white sand except where those rocks crop out half a mile from the near end. I could see a white spot on the rocks. It moved. Chust a sheep, thought I, but down I went none the less, through the dunes to the beach. The tide wass flooding. Says I to myself, "In another hour that sheep will be cut off." I searched the rocks and there at the farthest point sat a naked woman. Her back wass turned to me and her lower half in the water.'

'How could you tell it wass a wuman?' asked Erchie briskly.

'Hair to the waist, man. Forbye, I could tell by the build: slender like a boy yet wide at the hips. I wass tip-toeing away when a thought struck me. There wass not a footprint on the sand behind the rocks, saving my own. Again, that lass had been sitting there maybe twenty meenutes, half in the water and half out—and her not feeling the cold on a May night! Not a sign of her clothes. Something funny here, thought I. So back I went and there she still wass, and what do you think she would be at? She wass combing her hair with a piece of shell, and that hair wass green even by moon-light.

'Says I to her soft-like and not to frighten her, "Come now, Miss, what iss all thiss? You will be catching your death if you stay here."

'She started round, showing me creatt violet eyes wide with surprise. "I am the polissman from Screavie," says I. "No need to be frightened of me, lass." But not a word said she. "It iss too cold for mortal wuman," I went on, "to be sitting here with not a stitch on. It will be hospital for you unless you come quick ashore." Still she made no answer, and the wind blowing chill off the sea. Her big dark eyes were looking me aal over, ass if I wass chust a horse at a fair. I began to feel angry. "Miss!" I commanded right sherp; "come you ashore and dress this instant, or I will be charging you with indecent exposure and loitering with intent."

'Quick as an eel, she slipped into the sea and away, not swumming, though the soles of her feet flicked the surface, but shooting off into deep water. I hung around the rocks for an hour. Not a soul came ashore.'

'Stop you!' cried Hamish Stewart the forester. 'If she had feet she wass no mermaid.'

'Och,' said old Murdo MacGregor the crofter, 'there iss different kinds or clesses of mermaid. Some haff legs and some tails, some haff green hair and some silver like the sands of Camus Ban. The mermen cannot live ashore, while mermaids can. Not enough iss known on the subchect. Research iss needed. Some young lad from Aberdeen University should be writing a thesis for his Ph.D.'

'How do you know aal this?' challenged Hamish.

'I haff seen them,' replied Murdo. 'Heuch, aye, often and often I see them when herding my sheep by Cnoc Ban. In spring and summer they come out of the water in daytime. Yess, now, I remember well that first time twenty years ago, when I wass rounding up for the clipping. I wass coming through the marram gress on the dunes when suddenly Jessie pointed, hackles up and snarling. This cannot be a ewe, thought I, and looked over a knoll to the beach. On the rocks lay a naked lass. Aye, and when I looked again I saw the tail, silvery green like her hair, chust as Niall says. Next year the same. This time there wass no tail, but a good pair of legs. Yet each time my dog gave a howl like a wolf and fled in terror, neffer heeding my whustle.'

'And the mermaids?' asked Niall. 'Did you neffer get any closer?'

'The instant the dogs howl they slip into the water and off. I haff sat on, but they neffer reappear. One thing they cannot bide iss dogs.'

'It iss not canny,' swore Niall. 'As long as I liff I will not be walking alone at night by the Camus Ban.'

In the midst of the joking that followed this statement, Rhuridh turned abruptly and stalked out of the bar. For a moment even mermaids were forgotten. Rhuridh gone without a word! How could this be? 'Och, he has gone to the Camus Ban to find himself a mermaid,' laughed old Murdo.

But that was just what Rhuridh did. With an unexpected force, the conversation in Meg's bar had set his mind in turmoil, as if the words had been destined for his ears alone, telling him something he was fated to hear. He could not think, for he did not know what to think; he could only feel. The earnest tone of voice used by Niall and Murdo, and their serious manner, had deeply impressed him. Mermaids! How could there be mermaids? Had they been in the ark? Many another creature had been in the ark and not listed. Then there was the dog's terror; no, mermaids could not have been in the ark with dogs. They must have swum alongside like dolphins. Marine ecologists believed them extinct, but maybe the men of the Ross and Sutherland coasts could show otherwise. Was it his vocation to lead the proofs? Or to convert mermaids to Christianity? Or what?

His excitement mounted as he crossed the dunes to the Camus Ban. He could hear at first only the near rustle of the marram grass round his legs, and the distant swish of the sea, growing louder as he drew near until the rhythmical roar of waves rushing up and down the sands drowned every other sound save one—the sudden thumping of his heart. A strange tumult of the blood was in Rhuridh MacAlpine. He had to stop and calm himself before peering round the last knoll to the beach. The Camus Ban stretched bare and empty under the moon.

A sad anticlimax that was. Search as he might that night —and he walked from end to end and back—not one trace of life could he see on sand or rock. Ten miles he covered on foot by the time he reached home, a cottage set in a stand of Scots pines, sited two hundred yards behind the manse. He lived alone, and thought to sleep well after his long walk, but instead of his usual deep untroubled sleep he suffered a restless night, tossing and dreaming of mermaids.

Next day was Saturday. To the wonderment of all, Rhuridh failed to appear that night at Meg's bar. He was down at the Camus Ban again. A high wind was blowing off the sea and mile-long waves creaming on the beach. 'If there iss such a thing ass mermaids,' said he to himself, 'this will be no night for the likes of them, when the sea roars and breakers crash on the rocks. I will come again chust once, and that will haff to be the end.'

On Sunday the skies opened wide and blue to a May heat-wave. At both morning and evening service Rhuridh was the first man into kirk and the last away. He took Sabbath school and bible class with a fiery eloquence that broke sweat on the palms of every sinner. He felt a need to fortify the spirit for the battle to come. At his home he devoted the rest of the daylight hours to meditation on the sea and its strange life, and when darkness fell made his way around Cnoc Ban. The night seemed black while he crossed the moorland, but lightened on the marram where the sand thickened under his feet. Suddenly the d...nes fell away. The full moon was rising out of the sea, gigantic and yellow as a haystack. He sat down at the edge of the beach and watched in wonder as it slowly rose, shrinking in size and whitening, flood-lighting sea and shore till the long miles of the Camus Ban shone like a snowfield. The beach lay desolate as ever, marked black only by the one outcrop of glistening rocks. The very air seemed charged with magic. Rhuridh covered the beach from end to end, at first walking, then taking off his shoes and socks to run barefoot at the wet sea's edge. The delight of freedom as he last knew it when a boy set his blood tingling. He ran in big circles, mad as a wild wolf under the moon, rejoicing in the soft air and sand and sea.

'My clothes are chust hampering me,' thought he, and stripped them off to run more freely still. His body felt glowing and alive. And the sea winked a glitter and whispered on flat sands, till its come-hither call could no longer be denied. He spun round and ran in near the rocks. He threw himself headlong and swam and swam, then came in to the farthest point of the outcrop. He heaved himself out on to a flat slab and looked up. His eyes met those of a young woman. A few feet above him, she was sitting on a ledge, examining him thoroughly. Well pleased she must have been with what she saw, for she smiled a smile to turn a man's heart, at once tender and friendly, yet bold. Under long silky lashes her eyes were huge and violet, dark as mid-ocean, alert as a bird's. She was naked and ready to plunge off that ledge as quick as a darting merganser.

Rhuridh blushed to the roots of his hair and would have jumped back into the sea had a thought not stopped him. The lass might have no tail, but her hair was a pale, pale green and fell to her hips. She had been combing it with a shell, which she still held in her hand.

'Are you a mermaid?' blurted Rhuridh in Gaelic, and blushed again, for the question did sound daft when spoken. This lass was real. But she did not smile again. She frowned and looked puzzled and asked a question herself—in a tongue foreign to Rhuridh. Her voice had the West High-

land lilt, but when Rhuridh tried her in the English she made
no answer. He tried again in Latin, Greek, and French, but
she knew none. Gradually Rhuridh came to realise the truth.
The lass was indeed a mermaid, of the two-legged variety,
and he had proof of it before the night was out.

Under his questions she grew more and more impatient,
and signed to him to come and sit beside her. Rhuridh was
suddenly embarrassed. He could not as soon as this get
over a life-long shyness of women. Amid the spate of his
questions, he had forgotten he had nothing on, and now
remembered and was ashamed, and half-turned away to
hide himself. 'Who told thee that thou wast naked?' The
words jumped to mind. This beautiful mermaid might be
living still in her Garden of Eden, all innocent, and not like
fallen Man. His spirits lifted wonderfully at the notion. A
mermaid was not a human. She was not just an animal,
either, nor yet a fish, but she was a creature of the deep
ocean. A man is not ashamed to be naked before an animal,
and likewise, thought Rhuridh, it is foolish to be ashamed
before a mermaid. The lightening of his heart was so sharp
and sudden that he felt ecstatic. He turned to her and held
out his arms. 'Come with me to the sands,' he commanded,
and waved an arm to the shore. She must have understood
the gesture, for she tripped blithely over the rocks behind
him.

The moment their feet touched the sand she came alongside and put her hand in his. The movement was so
spontaneous and trusting that Rhuridh went wild with joy.
'Let us run!' he cried, and they ran, hand in hand up the
beach to the dry sands. Rhuridh stopped and suggested
they sit down and try to communicate. Either she misunder-
stood or understood too well: she flung herself into his arms.
Involuntarily his arms went round her. Then he realised
what was happening and made to withdraw, but 'Och, she

iss not a human,' he reminded himself. 'She iss like a wee dog desiring affection—it would be shameful to speak sherp.' Just the same, since he now felt free of inhibition, her kiss fell sweeter on his mouth than any human's he had tasted. To save himself he had suddenly to lift her clear off the ground and set her gently down on the sand. He dropped beside her then and taking a fistful of sand let it run through his fingers, saying the word 'sand' over and over again and pointing. She understood at once and repeated, 'sand.' He pointed to his hand and to hers and said, 'hand.' In no time they were exchanging words so fast that soon Rhuridh had to halt, lest each forget them. The most important word he learned was her name, which sounded like Mairi.

Mairi had a far better memory than he. She forgot never a word he taught her. She loved the deep sound of his voice, and his curly hair. Her hand was ever up at the nape of his neck to feel it and to run her fingers through the rich red mop to the forehead and back. Her finger-tips sensed the man's virility under the silky whiteness of his skin, for they set every rope-like muscle a-quiver. The flat belly and narrow hips below his broad chest delighted her hand and eye. There was not a thing about him she did not like.

Rhuridh's mind was in a whirl, not knowing what to think. Overwhelmed by her tenderness, the like of which he had never known, wonderstruck by the perfect shape of the creature, same as a woman's but more lithe, firm, and supple, he surrendered to the joy of the moment. Her only difference from human likeness was her hair, and even that vanished as it dried, the green fading out to palest blonde. Above all else, what charmed Rhuridh was the unhesitating confidence she had in him, bold and free and quick in becoming intimate, because innocent as any creature of the wild. The deeper he looked into her violet eyes, the more engulfed he felt in their friendship and love. Hours passed like minutes, and dawn was near breaking when they rose to part. She accompanied him a quarter of a mile over the sands to his clothes, and stood astonished while he put them on. She had thought him a new kind of merman. She was heartbroken, yet felt a spurt of hope when he went down with her to the water's edge. She tried to lure him in, and when that failed, to pull him in. 'I will be coming tomorrow,' cried Rhuridh, resisting her, but she seemed not to understand. As the first light spread across the sky she gave a cry of despair and dived into the sea. So clear and still was the water that he could see her white body far out under the surface, streaking away like a fish, aye, and she never broke surface again, long as he watched.

Rhuridh found his soul in a turmoil that day. A man can be in love and still be teaching thirty boys and girls, but when Rhuridh's mind was not on the floor of the sea with Mairi it was wrestling with problems of moral theology. At lunchtime he had to dismiss the class for the day. Was a mermaid to be ranked as human or animal? Rhuridh had to know. In the Wee Free Kirk it is not lawful to make love to a beast of the field or a fish of the sea, nor even to a human before marriage. But Mairi was none of these things, and the Good Book spoke of no bar to marriage. The notion of wedding Mairi thus came to his mind for the first time, only to be put aside till marriage was seen to be possible, for Rhuridh was a practical man. He made a resolve. He would not give way again to the will of the flesh, and with this good intention went that night to the Camus Ban. He would teach Mairi enough English to understand his firm resolves. Then they could be good friends, and he would convert her to Christianity and to the way of the Wee Free Kirk. That would be his mission. Forbye, they would tell each other all about their different ways of life, and Rhuridh as a good scholar was afire to learn about Mairi's.

She was waiting as before at the far point of rock. He swam out and joined her. So beautiful and eager she was that before he knew she was in his arms and he carrying her ashore to the dry sand. Night after night through the month of May and early June this happened. The lessons would start always the same way. She would snuggle into his shoulder and give it a kiss and say 'shoulder,' then stroke his red beard and say 'beard,' and draw her fingers down his arm and say 'arm,' and so with all the rest of him, till there was no part of a man she did not know in English. In the same way she would introduce Rhuridh to herself, so that soon there was no part of a mermaid he did not know in Merman. Never had a man so enjoyed learning a new language, nor learned one so fast. By the time she had learned enough English to understand what his good intentions were, the good intentions had long since been by-passed. The hours in her company that once sped as minutes now flashed past like seconds.

Rhuridh was head over heels in love. Long before the end of May, the folk of Screavie were wondering what was ailing him. Great dark hollows were appearing under his eyes, and no longer did he call down hell-fire and damnation on poor sinners. Indeed, he never showed up on weekend nights at Meg's bar, and at bible class made no man's palms sweat with fear. Yet his eyes were alive and joyous. The women diagnosed the trouble straight away. 'The man iss in luff,' said they, 'you need chust look at him.' But few could really believe it—for where was the lass?

Sheila wept alone at her aunt's cottage at Liabaig.

What can man do when he loves a mermaid? Rhuridh knew: marry or burn. The problems might have beaten a lesser man than he, but Rhuridh could be practical if need were. He worked away at the English with Mairi. Under the stars of mid-summer's night he asked the lass to marry him, and to live with him. He revealed the difficulties she would have to face.

'Mairi wear clothes—neffer!' she gasped. 'Life in house choke me—walls too near, too dry, too warm. . . . Oh, Rhuridh, oh darling one, I luff you! I come if you say "Come." I will be wife and luff you daytime, nighttime, aaltime. Neffer will there be moment we not make luff.'

They lay in each other's arms near the dunes and all seemed easy. 'Let me take you home tonight,' urged Rhuridh. 'I will hide you there till I can go to Inverness and buy clothes, and till you learn how to use tables and chairs, and knives and forks, and fires and so on.'

'I tremble,' whispered Mairi. 'I fright. Fires! . . . Och, with you I will be safe, my beluffed, my dear one. I come.'

At one o'clock in the morning they stole off to Screavie. Mairi could walk through the marram grass, but her feet were too tender for the moor. Rhuridh had to carry her from there all the way home. His relief was immense when the cottage pleased her. First of all delights was the bath and shower, then the mirrors, the carpets, and the glass in the windows. Nothing would persuade her to lay hand on the electric cooker and fires.

They went to bed and fell asleep in each other's arms. At six o'clock in the morning Rhuridh woke up to find Mairi gone. He jumped up in a panic and rushed to search the house. She was asleep in the bath and it full to the brim. And so it was every night after that: she would stay in bed with Rhuridh till he fell asleep, then away she'd steal to her natural element next door. There was no curing her. She could not sleep between sheets.

At breakfast that morning she would not touch the

porridge or bacon, but luckily Rhuridh had a fish in the house. Later she learned to drink milk, and develop a taste for poached egg. She would eat no meat or potatoes and sighed for seaweed. As the days went by Rhuridh was sore put about to feed her. Erchie MacFarlane sold him fish, but more variety was needed. When Saturday came at last, he went off to Inverness and bought the lass clothes. For Rhuridh that was torment, standing about in milliners' shops, selecting ladies' underwear, while the shop-girls eyed him strangely, and he terrified that someone he knew might open the door. He took everything home in two suitcases, one full of clothes and the other sea-food. In the end it was worth it. Mairi danced with joy when she saw the contents. A meal came first: mussel soup, scampi, and lemon sole. The rest of the night passed in front of a mirror, the pair of them nearly helpless with laughter. All the clothes were like fancy dress on Mairi.

At eleven o'clock, when darkness was falling, they ventured out for the first time together and made straight for the Camus Ban. It seemed just like old times when they stripped off and ran over the sands. Mairi carried a basket, in which she gathered the seaweeds she wanted. Every night in fine weather they came here. In the daylight hours she taught herself to write, but never could she put her nose out of doors, and this fretted her. After the first days of wearing clothes she would suffer them no longer. Rhuridh would come home from school to find her romping naked round the house. He tried to insist on her wearing clothes: she must get used to them, said he, and not scandalise the folk of Screavie in days to come. This led to quarrels ('But Rhuridh, darling, why should I hide myself in cloth?'), and to tears, and to reconciliations in bed, but the strain was mounting. She would not obey him long in anything if her mind was different. Rhuridh came to realise that all her life she had been free as the waves and wind, and nothing could change her now.

Her saving graces were many. She could laugh. Beautiful, intelligent, and gay, she could rouse his love at a moment's notice, prolong it for hours, and give him his heart's desire. Rhuridh was a happy man and sought only the best ways and means to arrange a marriage for August. Meantime, great caution was needed. The advanced bible class, which was the one Sheila attended, still met in his house on Wednesdays. When they came, Mairi kept to the bedroom and all evidence was carefully removed from other rooms. In July, the minister was away for his summer holidays and the manse closed. The Women's Guild, who always met on Wednesday evenings at the manse, asked Rhuridh if they could come to his house instead, so that they could have tea with their knitting. He told them to come at eight, when the bible class ended, and warned Mairi to keep fast to her room till he sounded the gong in the hall, which was their long-agreed sign that the coast was clear.

The bible class that night were hoping that the old, volcanic Rhuridh might erupt just once again. There was fire in his eye, but from his nostrils came no smoke, no flame, and no steam. His voice, low, growling, and subdued, read to them from the Song of Solomon. The lasses did not know where to look. He put down the Good Book. 'What iss luff?' he asked. 'Tell me.' He waited. No one dared to answer.

With no warning the new Rhuridh erupted. 'Luff or be damned!' he shouted. 'Learn to luff or you wither like grass in the oven! Who iss your beluffed? Choose her! Find him! You sit like cows looking over a fence when you should be chumping over the moon!' He gave it them hot and strong till their palms sweated as of old——but what a change, what a transformation of the man!——no word of devils stabbing

141

sinners with pitch-forks. He had forgotten all about time. The Women's Guild assembling on his doorstep opened the front door and filed into the hall. Janet Dunbar from Castle Ross was there, and Jean MacPherson, and Fiona Munro, and Wullie the Post's wife, and others. When they heard Rhuridh's bass voice blasting like a storm on the Minch they stopped. They listened at the sitting-room door. But on he went.

'The man has recovered his speerits, I'm glad to hear,' said Janet, short-like. 'But time iss getting on,' and turning to the gong she gave it half a dozen belts with the hammer. Rhuridh's voice cut off short. In they marched to the sitting-room. He was standing there with his jaw dropped, white in the face and staring at a door on the opposite side of the room. He made a sudden rush at it—but too late. It burst open and Mairi danced in naked, crying, 'Rhuridh, my beluffed, my darling!'

She stopped dead. Head and breasts held high, white arms outstretched, hair flowing to the hips and shining like wind-silvered barley, she stood poised there a long, long moment, transfixed by the arrow-eyes of a dozen women. Then with a frightened cry she threw herself into Rhuridh's arms.

Sheila fled out of the house. Fiona Munro, the greatest sinner of them all, the one who would quickest have taken Rhuridh for lover, gave tongue first. 'The Weemen's Guild,' she said in icy tones, 'meets in a den of fice.'

'We see Satan Himself, stripped of sheep's clothing,' remarked Janet, dead-pan.

'And him a teacher with bairns in his care!' cried Wullie the Post's wife.

'And my wee Cheanie one of them!' cried another.

'Think black burning shame on you, Rhuridh MacAlpine.' Their tongues were loose like steel dirks and Rhuridh left them to it. He picked Mairi up and carried her through to the bedroom. He laid her gently on the bed and slowly kissed away the tears streaming from her violet eyes. Then he strode back to the sitting-room cackle. 'Out of this house!' he roared just once. The very foundations shook to it. The ladies jumped like shot hens and some ran, others eyed him scornfully and nose in air stalked out, but none dared wait to argue. His face was black with rage. They had hurt his Mairi! How could she ever meet them again? Or pretend to be like them? What kind of life could she hope for in Screavie?

And well Mairi understood what had happened. Her shoulders were heaving with sobs when Rhuridh hastened back to her. 'Becoss of me,' she wept, 'you will loss chob and drown in hate of weemens.' She sat up with sudden decision. 'Let us go to the Camus Ban. There it iss clean and good.' They rose and went.

No moon shone but the stars were bright and the sand still warm from the day's sun. In long frizzy lines the waves hissed gently over the lower beach. They swam to cleanse themselves of the Women's Guild, and then to be whole and well again made love on the warm sands by the dunes. Rhuridh fell asleep in Mairi's arms, and awoke in the early hours to find her gone. When he sat up he saw written in the sands, *I go to my people. Do not look for me. Do not wait—I not come again. I love you. Mairi.*

He sprang up with a great cry, 'Mairi!' and ran to the sea's edge. Her line of footprints went all the way, newly crumbling where the sea swept wafer-thin. He never saw her again.

Night after night Rhuridh went back to the Camus Ban, watching for long hours a sea violet as Mairi's eyes, and stretching empty to the rim of the world. At first he watched in hope, then in despair, yet at the last fully awake—awake to his need of a woman's love and tenderness.

After long weeks of waiting he began to wonder if Mairi had ever existed in reality, or if somehow he had taken leave of his senses for a space, and imagined her presence or dreamed it. That someone had taught him much would be hard to deny. For in the end he went back to Sheila, she of the hair black as a Lewis bog and skin smooth as a copper birch. The tongues of the Women's Guild made no clack, nor did Sheila herself ever utter one word of reproach. On the day they wed, the new Rhuridh was a man she could love as never the old. And many a thing she learned from him, which he could never have known but for Mairi.

THE HEBRIDES

W. H. Murray

'There have been many books about the islands which ring the west coast of Scotland but none of the standard of W. H. Murray's . . . he brings to it a deep understanding and a remarkable knowledge. He is geologist, historian, ornithologist, botanist, topographer and sociologist all in one. Coupled to this is the skill of a graphic writer.'

Scottish Field

'. . . must be placed firmly among the best accounts ever given of the islands. . . . He deals with all the inhabited islands and gives a wealth of practical information about each, some of it surprising, perhaps, for those who do not know the Hebrides.'—*Daily Telegraph*

'Mr W. H. Murray is a most distinguished writer on the Scottish rural scene. . . . He clearly loves the Hebrides but, what is more important, knows them extremely well—indeed in extraordinary detail. . . . It is refreshing to come across a book about these 500 and more islands in which the flesh of affection is supported by the hard bones and skeleton of verified fact.'—*Irish Times*

16 pp. of photographs   14 maps